MATTHEW SWANSON & ROBBI BEHR

the REAL McCoys

[Imprint]
MAKE YOUR MARK

NEW YORK

To Jesse, who introduced us to Erin, who gave us the chance of a lifetime.
To Bridget, who introduced us to Meredith, who filled our hearts with Moxie.

SQUARE FISH

An imprint of Macmillan Publishing Group, LLC
175 Fifth Avenue
New York, NY 10010
mackids.com

Our books may be purchased in bulk for promotional, educational, or business use. Please contact your local
bookseller or the Macmillan Corporate and Premium Sales Department at (800) 221-7945 ext. 5442 or
by e-mail at MacmillanSpecialMarkets@macmillan.com.

Library of Congress Cataloging-in-Publication Data

Names: Swanson, Matthew, 1974- author. | Behr, Robbi, illustrator.
Title: The real McCoys / by Matthew Swanson ; illustrated by Robbi Behr.
Description: New York : Imprint, 2017. | Summary: Elementary school detective Moxie McCoy looks for a
    missing school mascot and a new best friend, with the help of her annoying little brother. | Description
    based on print version record and CIP data provided by publisher; resource not viewed.
Identifiers: LCCN 2016050389 (print) | LCCN 2017022328 (ebook) | ISBN 9781250098542
    (Ebook) | ISBN 9781250098528 (hardcover) | ISBN 9781250098535 (paperback)
Subjects: | CYAC: Mystery and detective stories. | Brothers and sisters—Fiction. |
    Detectives—Fiction. | Schools—Fiction.
Classification: LCC PZ7.S9719 (ebook) | LCC PZ7.S9719 Re 2017 (print) |
    DDC [Fic]—dc23
LC record available at https://lccn.loc.gov/2016050389

[Imprint]
MAKE YOUR MARK

@ImprintReads
Originally published in the United States by Imprint
First Square Fish Edition: 2018
Book designed by Robbi Behr and Natalie C. Sousa
Square Fish logo designed by Filomena Tuosto
Imprint logo designed by Amanda Spielman

10 9 8 7 6 5 4 3 2

AR: 5.2 / LEXILE: 830L

This is the story of a sister and brother,
Two opposite thinkers who need one another,
To rescue an owl and capture a crook.
I won't tell you how. That's the point of the book.
But when you're done reading (there's no way around it),
Please put this book on the shelf where you found it.
For if you should steal it, the fate you'd enjoy
Is facing the wrath of one Moxie McCoy.

PROLOGUE

The name's Moxie. Moxie McCoy. If you didn't know already, *Moxie* means "force of character." It means "ultimate determination." It means "death-defying nerve."

In other words, you have been warned.

I am ten years old. I am in fourth grade. I go to

TIDDLYWHUMP ELEMENTARY SCHOOL.

And that is all you need to know about me. At least, that's all you *get* to know. I like to be a little bit mysterious, thank you very much. It helps me do what I do.

And what do I do?

I solve problems, of course.

Favorite notebook missing?

I will find it.

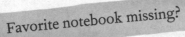

Someone took your lunch money?

I'm on it.

Think you might be the long-lost heir

of a legendary British earl

and need definitive proof?

I live for the challenge.

I have been trained by the *best of the best*, by which I mean
Annabelle Adams, Girl Detective, protector of justice
and thwarter of all things menacing or unpleasant.
Annabelle's thrilling adventures contain the
solution to any problem, and I have read all 58
books in the series 37½ times. What Annabelle
knows, I know. And Annabelle knows *everything*.

But I'm getting ahead of myself. This story hasn't actually started yet. So why am I telling you this?

Because sometimes it's nice to have a taste of dessert *before* you start your dinner.

The littlest nibble of double-fudge brownie or the smallest scoop of ice cream.

To get you through the salad and the meat loaf and the soup. To let you know the *good* stuff's on its way.

3

CHAPTER 1: MAKING A LIST

It is Friday, December 18th. It is 12:37 a.m. I am not asleep, because I am making a list of questions to use when interviewing new best friend candidates.

My old best friend is Maude. She is fascinating and beautiful and speaks Korean. Her hair is black, her eyes are gray, and she gets a triple dimple when she smiles.

Utterly amazing things about *Maude*:

- Rides a unicycle
- Hates soup
- Loves avocados
- Adores slugs
- Can hit a bottle with a slingshot from 50 paces
- Appreciates the mellow timbre of a well-played flügelhorn
- Can put her left leg behind her head (but, for some reason, not her right one!)

Maude recently moved to California, and I'm not sure my life will be possible without her. I tried to explain this to her mom and dad, but they refused to listen.

We were the perfect problem-solving duo, known to clients and enemies alike as  I was the muscle, and Maude was the brains. I collected clues, and she connected dots. Our work was legendary, as in:

> *The Case of the Missing Lunch Box,*
> *The Riddle of the Great Big Pile*
> *of Whiteboard Erasers,* and
> *The Confusing Situation Involving*
> *Two Blond Boys Named Donald.*

We were respected. We were feared. There was no problem we couldn't handle when we put our heads together.

Since Maude left town, the cases take longer to solve and are only half as fun. Choosing her replacement is perhaps the most important decision I will ever make, and I need to get it right.

And so I am making a list.

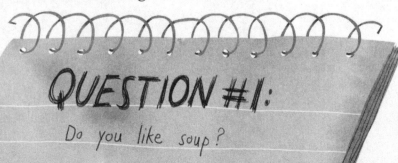

QUESTION #1:

Do you like soup?

One day in kindergarten, they served us chicken noodle soup for lunch. But because soup of any kind is watery and horrible, both Maude and I cried so hard that Mrs. Swellingrove sent us to the nurse's office to calm down.

There, on the nurse's bench, with snot running from our puffy red noses, Maude and I agreed we would be best friends forever.

QUESTION #2:

How do you feel about avocados?
(extra credit for mentioning guacamole)

I had my first bite of guacamole on a blue corn chip at Maude's house one day in first grade, and since that electrifying moment, my life has never been the same.

Avocados are special to me in the way that birthdays and water balloons and really ripe peaches are special to me.

Having a best friend who doesn't like avocados would be like having a dentist who doesn't like washing his hands before sticking them in your mouth.

QUESTION #3:

Which are better: marshmallows or slugs?
(should be obvious)

After every rainstorm, Maude and I would go outside and look for slugs on drainpipes and fence posts.

Because both of us agree that slugs are beautiful, remarkable creatures that get a bad reputation on account of being slimy.

Marshmallows, on the other hand, are only slightly less awful than soup. Maude and I do not understand how blobby chunks of sugary fluff can create such excitement. The person who invented them is surely laughing somewhere.

QUESTION #4:

Can you ride a unicycle?
(bonus points for eyes closed)

When we were in second grade, Maude begged her parents for a unicycle, then practiced for a year until she could ride it forward and backward with her eyes closed. Try as I might, I cannot do it.

Not forward.

Not backward.

Not even with my eyes open.

If Maude wanted to, she could be a professional unicyclist. But she plans to be a pediatric oncologist.

As I read through the list, my heart sinks to the bottom of the ocean in my chest.

Trying to find another Maude van den Cloot is like trying to take a nap while riding on the back of a galloping rhinoceros.

9

CHAPTER 2: OH BROTHER

Suddenly, it's morning. I do twenty jumping jacks. I touch my toes a hundred times. I spend precisely twenty minutes reading Annabelle Adams, Girl Detective, Volume 32:

It's the one where Annabelle becomes a *double* agent, then a *triple* agent, and then (surprise!) a *quadruple* agent.

By the end, everyone else is so confused that no one knows who Annabelle works for but Annabelle—who was actually a *quintuple* agent all along.

While all the senators and archaeologists stand around shouting, she finds the critical clue (a dirty gym sock!) that basically unravels the *entire* mystery, jumps out of a flaming helicopter, lands on the head of the 100-foot statue of King Whiplash III, and discovers the stolen blueprints of the

MEGABIT ROBOTIC ELBOW

(in the statue's left nostril, of course), thwarting her nemesis, Dr. Fungo, and his evil plot to conquer the pointy part of

IDAHO!

I reread Annabelle's adventures each and every morning because (1) I love them, (2) Annabelle is my hero and Maude's hero, and (3) Maude and I spend every day at recess discussing Annabelle's techniques and using them to solve our clients' problems. At least we *used* to, before Maude moved to California and left me in misery.

After reading, I go downstairs and eat two bowls of oatmeal (power for the brain) and do a crossword puzzle.

My little brother, Milton, shows up, pours himself a bowl of Atomic Nut Bombs, and starts reading an enormous book called *Gods of Ancient Rome*.

It's the kind of book you'd read in *middle school*. Milton is in *first grade*.

I have to admit, his brain is a marvel, but I never tell him that. If his head gets any bigger, we'll need a new house.

Happenstance, says Milton.

What?

Another word for "coincidence," he says.

Nine down. Happenstance.

It is the crossword clue I have been working on. I did not ask for help. Milton has an unpleasant way of answering questions *before* they are asked.

You didn't even *look*!

I read it yesterday.

He says it with his mouth full, which he knows is impolite and also a choking hazard.

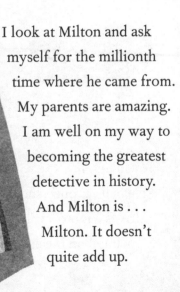

I look at Milton and ask myself for the millionth time where he came from. My parents are amazing. I am well on my way to becoming the greatest detective in history. And Milton is . . . Milton. It doesn't quite add up.

Dad works at the bicycle factory. His hands are strong from pulling levers all day. He has read every book in the library.

He has been to every single state.

He can juggle five balls at once and drives a motorcycle with a blue flame painted on the side.

Mom is an entomologist who travels all over the world. Right now she is in the Amazon rain forest discovering new kinds of insects in the tallest trees. She is probably a spy.   And possibly a samurai.

But this is **CLASSIFIED** information.

You are probably wondering if she ever named an insect after me, and the answer is "of course she did" and probably will again. It's called the *Moximaxus*, and it eats other bugs for lunch, and it has bright green spots on its proboscis, which is a part of an insect's mouth, if you didn't already know.

Milton, on the other hand . . .

is like a turtle mixed
with a watermelon
mixed with a pile
of pinecones.

WATERMELON

TURTLE

PILE OF
PINECONES →

And by that I mean he moves really slowly, has a great
big head, and never has anything interesting to say. He
follows every rule. He chews each bite of food 30 times
before swallowing it.

   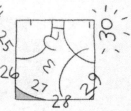

And he's the shortest kid in his class by about four inches.

It seems almost impossible that Milton
could be my *actual* brother.

I sometimes wonder if he might have been left on our doorstep by a family of aliens from a planet so boring that no one wants to raise their kids there.

Because my parents are just the sort of kind and remarkable people who would be willing to take in an uninspiring alien baby and raise him as their own—even if he could never be a *real* McCoy.

Dad shows up and fixes himself some eggs.

Status report?

Six dreams.

Good ones?

Four good, two bad.

One bad dream had been about Maude leaving town, and the other had been about otters. Even though they are extremely cute, otters have always worried me.

"That's progress," he says, munching his toast.

"Yep," I say. When Maude first moved, pretty much *all* my dreams were bad.

"How about you, friend?" asks Dad, kissing the top of Milton's head.

Milton doesn't like to talk about his dreams.

"When's Mom coming home?" he asks, trying to change the subject.

"You know the answer," says Dad.

Mom won't be home in time for Christmas. She is very close to discovering a brand-new bug. She has recently found its poop, which is green and iridescent and not like any poop she's seen before, but she hasn't found the bug itself. So she has to follow the poop trail while the poop trail is hot.

As a problem solver myself, I understand this. Sometimes sacrifices must be made in the name of the greater good. But it really bothers Milton—I can tell.

The phone rings. It's Mom, calling for her morning hello. Dad says a bunch of gooey stuff, and then Milton "talks" to her for a few minutes.

uh-huh. yup. yes. yep.

Then it's my turn. These morning chats with Mom are the best part of my day.

Morning, Slim.

Slim is my detective name. It inspires fear in the heart of my enemies and love in the heart of my mom.

"Morning," I say.

"How is your list of questions coming?"

"Making progress," I say. "I'm about to start interviewing candidates."

"Don't be too hard on the applicants."

"I'll let you know how it goes."

"Listen," she says, "I need you to do me a favor."

"Anything," I say, because I would literally do *anything* for this amazing person who grew me from nothing in her belly, wiped my bottom for 2.67 years, and named a bug after me.

"I need you to keep an eye on Milton," she says. "He seems sad."

I had been hoping she was going to ask me to infiltrate a heavily guarded fortress, but I can tell from her voice that she's actually worried.

He really looks up to you.

Okay.

I'm on it.

I love you, says Mom.

I say it back.

As I hang up the phone, Milton looks up at the clock and panics.

It's time to go!

he cries, knocking over his orange juice, which he now has to clean up, which makes him panic more.

We have plenty of time, but Milton likes to get to school *really* early.

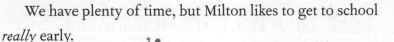

Just in case
a sinkhole
opens up in
the sidewalk

or dinosaurs attack

or a comet obliterates the
bridge over Ample Creek,
for example.

Usually, I like to give him a hard time about it by chewing my breakfast *really* slowly or pretending that my shoes have been stapled to the floor. But today I put on my coat and boots more quickly than usual.

And before you accuse me of getting soft, it's because I also want to get to school early today—for reasons that will become clear as soon as I feel like sharing them with you.

CHAPTER 3: MEET THE DUBLINGERS

Dad's rule is that Milton has to walk beside me
until we can actually see the school. So the moment
we turn the corner of Maple and Lark and the
magnificent shape of Tiddlywhump Elementary
comes into view, Milton sprints for the front door.

The bell won't ring for ⟨20 MINUTES⟩ but he likes to play it safe.

As I walk up the path to the school, I'm on the lookout
for best friend candidates. But I find myself less than
enthusiastic about the options. Everyone is acting like
an elementary school student. No one is talking about
the *important* things in life—like catching criminals
or rescuing kidnapped duchesses or negotiating secret
treaties between rogue nations. Instead, I hear talk of

PONIES, BASEBALLS, BARBIE DOLLS, and CARTOON MOVIES!

But as I go inside, I hear a boy named Brian and a
girl named Gwen talking about the winter assembly.

Today is the last day of school before winter break. Which means today is the day that the award winners will be announced. At the end of every term, Principal Jones gives out awards to the kids who have been the best in various ways.

And I am the best in various ways.

First there is

the Wise Owl Award,

which goes to the student with the best grades. While I agree that knowledge is as important as lightning-fast reflexes, I'm usually too busy battling the forces of injustice to worry about such minor details as *grades*.

I'm not interested in the Wise Owl Award and never will be.

Second is the Golden Owl Award, which goes to the student with the most Owl Points. Let me explain: Each of us starts the year with 100 Owl Points, but we lose one every time we break a rule.

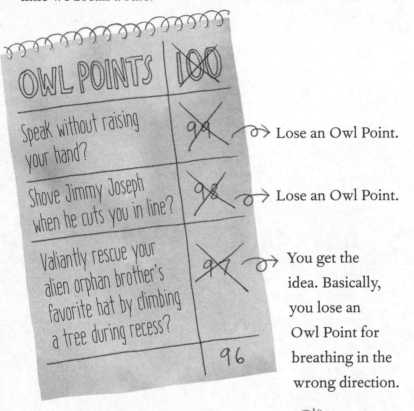

OWL POINTS	~~100~~	
Speak without raising your hand?	~~99~~	→ Lose an Owl Point.
Shove Jimmy Joseph when he cuts you in line?	~~98~~	→ Lose an Owl Point.
Valiantly rescue your alien orphan brother's favorite hat by climbing a tree during recess?	~~97~~	→ You get the idea. Basically, you lose an Owl Point for breathing in the wrong direction.
	96	

On the other side of the lobby, Milton is being interviewed by Dud Boggs, an extremely tall sixth grader who is one of the reporters for our school newspaper, the *Monthly Owl*.

The interview doesn't seem to be going very well, mostly because Milton refuses to speak. But Dud keeps asking questions and writing down notes. Perhaps the article will end up being a colorful description of Milton's gigantic head.

Milton is a little bit famous at the moment because he is tied for first place in the Owl Point standings with a second grader named Tiffany Eiffenbach. Both of them still have all 100 points, which is, quite frankly, astonishing. No one has ever won the Golden Owl with all 100 Owl Points. And there has never been a tie. We have no idea what Principal Jones is going to do. There is only *one* Golden Owl trophy. The winner gets to hold it for five minutes, and then it goes back in the case with our beloved mascot, Eddie the great horned owl.

Of course, Eddie is not a *real* great horned owl. That would be so mean. Eddie is like an owl-shaped teddy bear. He is fuzzy and brown and has a monocle and a tiny blue bow tie. He sits in a glass case in the school lobby. At the base of his case is a little sign that reads **Be wise like Eddie.**

That's basically our #1 responsibility at Tiddlywhump Elementary—to be wise like Eddie. Because what is greater than being wise? Nothing, that's what. Unless it is being *right*.

I walk over to Eddie's case and spend a minute just smiling at him (in spite of my general preference to look stern and mysterious). There has never been a finer mascot in the history of elementary school.

Which is why the last award, the Eddie Award, is so important. It goes to the student who has best lived up to Eddie's ideals of courage, patience, and wisdom—which, as everyone knows, is way more important than getting good grades or following every ridiculous rule every minute of the day.

I will almost *certainly* win the
Eddie Award because I am extremely
courageous, patient, and wise, and I
also have an insect named after me.
Please try not to be too shocked, but
I have been here for four and a half
years now and have never won it.
Maude won it twice, and she and
I are basically identical.

Even though I love Maude dearly and miss her terribly
and wish the best for her always, her being in California
increases my chances of winning by about 500%.

So it only makes sense that today is the day
when I will win and get my face added to the

WALL OF HONOR

outside the principal's office.
You may wish me luck, but I
frankly do not need it.

I'm still standing by Eddie's case, when our school custodian, Mr. Hammer, comes over and starts wiping down the glass.

Mornin', Slim. And how are things at M&M Inc.?

Good morning, Marvin.

Mr. Hammer is one of the few grown-ups who will actually call me Slim or who knows anything about my detective agency. And he is one of the few grown-ups who lets me call him by his first name.

One of the M's moved to California, and our caseload is a little light. But I have a feeling in my gut that the next big mystery is right around the corner.

That's good to hear. It's a big day for all of us. Got to get Eddie's case all spiffed up.

Will you be at the assembly?

Wouldn't miss it.

I suddenly wonder whether I should mention Mr. Hammer in my Eddie Award acceptance speech.

I really like Mr. Hammer. He's easygoing and seems very smart. I know that grown-ups and fourth graders are not usually best friends, but I also get the sense that if I want to find a suitable replacement for Maude, I'm going to have to think outside the box. So I take out my notebook and consult my list of questions.

"Do you like soup?" I ask.

"Sure do," he says with a smile.

I am discouraged. But not defeated. After all, as difficult as it is for me to believe, most people *do* like soup. I press on.

"What about avocados?" I say, squinting a bit to let him know that the question is very important.

"I like guacamole," he says. "Does that count?"

"Of *course* it does," I say. As far as I'm concerned, guacamole is basically just an avocado that fulfilled its destiny. He gets extra points.

"Next . . . which one is better: marshmallows or slugs?"

"Don't like marshmallows," he says, and my heart lifts.

I have found a sensible person at last.

"And I can't stand slugs. So slimy."
I put away my notebook.

"I'm afraid I disagree with you on that one, Marvin," I say. "But I respect your opinion."

And I do. Mr. Hammer is entitled to think whatever he wants about slugs. It's just that, in this case, he happens to be wrong.

I leave him to his cleaning and glance over at the other side of the lobby, where Tammy and Tracy Dublinger are selling

Together, the Dublingers have won the past six Wise Owl Awards. They are tied at three each, and neither one of them is happy about it.

Tammy is better at spelling.

c-t-h-u-l-h-u

Tracy is better at math.

$a^2 + b^2 = c^2$

Tammy is a little bit smarter.

Tracy is a little bit meaner.

Today will be the tiebreaker, putting one Dublinger firmly ahead of the other in the race to be the most obnoxious know-it-all in the universe. How will it play out? Personally, I don't give a flying fajita.

I take a deep breath as I walk up to their table. The Dublingers are about as lovable as the bumps on the end of an alligator's nose. But Mom is always encouraging me to "keep an open mind." And because Mom is wise and *almost* always right, I pause for a moment to ask myself whether one of the Dublingers might be new best friend material, even if only in some parallel universe.

But three seconds later, one of them opens her mouth, and my mind slams shut again.

FREE SAMPLES !!!

says a Dublinger with a voice so sharp and shrill it could cut through a telephone pole. I cannot tell which Dublinger it is, because they insist on dressing exactly the same.

"No thanks," I say.

"I wasn't talking to you, *Moxie*," says Tracy. I suddenly realize it's Tracy, because she's wearing a name tag that says HI, MY NAME IS TRACY.

I have instructed Tracy Dublinger approximately 1,000 times to call me Slim. The fact that she refuses to do it is one of approximately 1,000 things I do not like about her.

Don't get me wrong. I like my name. I *love* my name, in fact. Because it *means* something.

MOXIE is a kind of old-fashioned soda pop that Mom drank growing up and bought for Dad on their very first date.

Mom says she had to make sure he liked the taste of it because it was just like her— the perfect blend of bitter and sweet.

Dad says he knew after just one sip that he wanted to marry Mom. Though he didn't tell her this until a few years later so that he wouldn't seem like the kind of person who jumps to hasty conclusions.

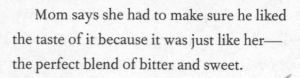

MOXIE might be the greatest name in the known universe. But every great detective needs a great detective nickname that strikes fear in the heart of her nemesis. And my nemesis is the one and only Tracy Dublinger.

"The name's *Slim*," I say.

"I wouldn't call you *Slim* even if Tammy's sweater were on fire and calling you Slim were the only way to put it out," says Tracy, letting out a laugh at the exact same time and at the exact same pitch as Tammy.

It doesn't seem like a very sisterly thing to say, and I wonder why Tammy finds it funny—but not for long, because now it's *her* turn to insult me.

"I wouldn't call you Slim if you asked really nicely and said please." Tammy lets out another awful laugh, but then stops suddenly when she realizes that Tracy isn't laughing with her. Instead, Tracy is looking at her twin as if Tammy were a bunny who just walked into a room full of cobras.

 That wasn't funny,

says Tracy with a sneer.

Really? I thought it was,

says Tammy.

 Not even a little.

Wait, are you sure?

 With zero doubt.

I leave them to their sibling warfare, giving a good loud

HHARRUMMPH!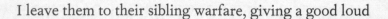

as I walk away to remind anyone who might happen to be listening that I do not like Wonder Scout Cookies because I do not like Wonder Scouts because I do not like Tammy or Tracy Dublinger. As I walk down the hallway to my classroom, everyone is still chattering about the assembly, the awards, and, most of all, the tie in the Golden Owl standings. Of course, all I want to do is go straight to the auditorium so that I can collect my Eddie Award at this very moment, but the assembly happens at the *end* of the day.

For the time being, I must spend a long and miserable stretch of hours at the mercy of my *other* nemesis.

CHAPTER 4: NEW BEST FRIEND CANDIDATES

My teacher, Mrs. Bunyan, might be the oldest person in the entire world. Some kids say she once met George Washington.

She has curly gray hair and old-fashioned glasses she might have purchased at a costume shop. She is not short and not tall and is kind of roundish and also kind of bony, and looks as if she might break in two at any moment. But she does not break in two. In spite of how she looks, Mrs. Bunyan is strong and tough and never gets tired of talking about pronouns, Eleanor Roosevelt, or Roman Numerals.

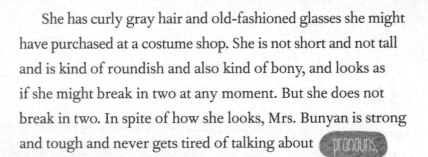

In case you are wondering, Mrs. Bunyan is *not* the kind of person who enjoys being hugged. In fact, she is exactly the kind of person who *doesn't*. We know because one time Veronica Parker tried it on a dare and ended up losing an Owl Point.

"Class!" snaps Mrs. Bunyan. "As you all know, the end-of-term spelling test will happen later this morning—right after recess."

I see Tammy and Tracy glance at each other

NERVOUSLY.

They are so close in the Wise Owl standings that even a single tricky silent letter might make all the difference.

Mrs. Bunyan continues, "But to get the day started on a productive and positive note, I'd like to talk for a while about *dental hygiene*."

There is a groan, an actual groan, from all of us together at once. Mrs. Bunyan doesn't seem to notice or care.

"If you will direct your attention to the front of the room . . ." she says, pulling out an enormous drawing of a mouth full of sickly yellowish teeth that someone has definitely not been brushing.

As Mrs. Bunyan does her best to save our mouths from the perils of sugary treats, I glance around at my classmates, trying so hard to keep my mind open, searching for even the faintest glimmer of hope that there is a new best friend among them.

To my left sits Bob Tuttleman, a tall boy with curly dark hair, endless energy, and a smile stuck on his face wherever he goes. He is literally bouncing up and down in his seat.

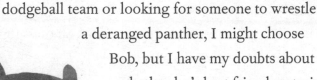

I admire Bob's enthusiasm. If I were putting together a dodgeball team or looking for someone to wrestle a deranged panther, I might choose Bob, but I have my doubts about whether he's best friend material. Still, given the lack of options, I make a mental note to ask him how he feels about soup at the next opportunity.

Across the room, Tammy and Tracy Dublinger are sitting there not saying anything while obviously having a hilarious silent conversation with their secret twin mind powers.

Even if they answered all four questions on my list with flying colors, I would never in 6,000 years invite them over for strawberry milk shakes.

☑ Yes.

☑ Yes.

☑ Yes.

NO!!

39

Unless, of course, it was a trick, as in Annabelle Adams, Girl Detective, Volume 17: *Bottoms Up*, when Annabelle dupes her nemesis, Dr. Fungo, into drinking what he *thinks* is a delicious milk shake but is actually Elmer's glue.

His mouth gets so clogged up with sticky, nontoxic goop that he can't bark orders to his army of menacing henchmen.

In the confusion that follows, Annabelle defeats all 10,000 of them using nothing but an overripe banana and a pair of left-handed sewing scissors.

Which is to say, there are certain limited circumstances in which I might offer a Dublinger something to drink.

Leon Magruder is sitting right in front of me, drawing furiously in his sketchbook. He has straight black hair and bird bones and a permanent hunch. All he does all day long is draw comics in which various superheroes punch and kick and shout at one another over and over again.

When Leon draws, it's a cross between drawing and actual fighting. He really gets into it. I feel sorry for the paper.

Could *Leon* be my new best friend? Perhaps. He's really smart. It's not a stretch to picture him on a unicycle. And he seems to care a lot about something, which is important to me. I have no idea whether he likes avocados, but one day at lunch I think I saw him eat a tub of something greenish that might have been guacamole . . . or spoiled potato salad.

I look across the room—

George Sandy Jamal Grace José Donna Freddie Veronica Chaz Elliot

The list goes on. Suddenly, it occurs to me. Not only are these my best friend candidates, but every single one of them is also potential competition for the Eddie Award.

Do any stand a chance?

I decide that none of them do.

Except . . . *perhaps* . . . the good and perfect Emily Estevez, who is . . . not at her desk, which is very strange, given that she is never late.

Emily won the Eddie Award in second grade and is *exactly* the kind of nice, considerate person who might win it again. Emily is also a potential new best friend candidate, assuming she is an actual fourth grader and not, as I occasionally suspect, a well-meaning cyborg or an undercover nun.

- She's smart (understands algebra).

x + y = z !

- She's strong (can do 40 push-ups).

- She's good (won the Golden Owl last year).

- *And* she's interesting (volunteers feeding elephants at the zoo).

Given my high standards and excellent taste, I suppose it makes perfect sense that my leading competition for the Eddie Award would also be at the top of my list of best friend candidates. *Does Emily like soup?* I am not sure. I do know from the talent show that she can play the recorder, but I have no idea if she also appreciates the flügelhorn.

I'm trying to remember if I've ever seen Emily eat a marshmallow, when Bob Tuttleman starts waving his hand.

Yes, Bob?

says Mrs. Bunyan, obviously irritated that she has to stop talking about gum disease.

I have to go to the bathroom,

says Bob.

Bob has to go to the bathroom a lot. And I mean a *lot*. You can tell that Mrs. Bunyan doesn't want to let him go. After all, leaving now would mean missing out on various important facts about his teeth.

But there is an ironclad Tiddlywhump rule that says teachers aren't allowed to say no if you ask to go to the bathroom. There was once a kid named Doug Doubletree who asked to go so often that the teachers stopped letting him, and then he peed in his pants in the art room and his mom came in to school and made a huge scene, and ever since then, if you say you have to go to the bathroom, the teachers *have* to let you. Even if they *really* don't want to. All because of Doug.

He's pretty much legendary.

Mrs. Bunyan gives Bob an irritated nod and hands him a bright green hall pass. He bounces out of the room like a giddy kangaroo.

I wish I'd thought of that! I'd give anything to be in the hall right now, away from Mrs. Bunyan and her tooth talk. I'd much rather be preparing my acceptance speech for when I win the Eddie Award.

Mrs. Bunyan returns to her lesson, but midway through a detailed description of root canals, the classroom door opens and best friend candidate Emily Estevez walks in, looking sleepy and a little sweaty.

Do you have a note?

I don't.

I fell asleep on the bus and just woke up.

I believe her. She has various sleeping-related dents on her face. Plus, Emily Estevez is so nice and good and perfect that she would never tell a lie.

> Did you stop at the front office and get a hall pass, at least?

asks Mrs. Bunyan.

> Of course.

Emily would sooner drown a kitten than break a single rule. She reaches into her pocket and then into her other pocket before realizing that she's all out of pockets and still can't find her hall pass.

Owl Points Lost
George – ꠸꠸꠸
Sandy – ꠸꠸꠸ ꠸꠸꠸
Jamal – ꠸꠸꠸ ꠸꠸꠸
Tracy – ꠸꠸
Emily – ꠸꠸
Elliott – ꠸꠸꠸ ꠸꠸꠸ ꠸꠸꠸
Chaz – ꠸꠸꠸ ꠸꠸꠸
Mofie – ꠸꠸꠸ ꠸꠸꠸ ꠸꠸꠸ ꠸꠸꠸
Veronica – ꠸꠸꠸
José – ꠸꠸꠸ ꠸꠸꠸

"I'm sorry, but that's one Owl Point!" sings Mrs. Bunyan with glee as she walks over to her secret teacher notebook where she keeps track of these things.

Mrs. Bunyan loves nothing more than taking away our Owl Points—even from the good and perfect Emily Estevez.

> 1. No Yawning.
> 2. No Stretching.
> 3. No smiling.
> 4. **NO JOY.**

I think she lies in bed at night and thinks up new rules for us to break.

Emily does not put up a fight. As she hangs her backpack on her hook, I notice it's bulging, as if everything she owns is crammed inside. The sequined elephant on the pocket looks like it's had way too much to eat, and the poor zipper seems like it might burst at any moment. Emily walks back to her desk, looking like she wants to cry or go back to sleep or crawl into a hole in the ground.

Mrs. Bunyan's enthusiastic explanation of gum health resumes, and I'm wishing I were anywhere but here, behind Leon, whose drawing has suddenly grown so loud and wild that I'm starting to worry a little. Apparently, his superheroes are in the middle of some epic battle. It sounds like he's sawing through the paper with his pencil.

I arch forward in my seat to get a better look. A muscle-bound guy with seven heads is battling a monster that looks like a unicorn mixed with an octopus mixed with a toaster.

Pow! shouts Leon. **Pow! Blam! Kazow!**

The other kids start to notice. Everyone is giggling, and soon Mrs. Bunyan realizes that most of us are missing important information about the dangers of plaque.

Leon.

Leon keeps POWing and BLAMing and KAZOWing.

Leon,

she says again, a little louder this time. Leon still doesn't notice. Which is kind of incredible, because now Mrs. Bunyan is standing right next to his desk, staring down like a thunderstorm that is about to rain all over him.

LEON!

Suddenly, Leon returns from whatever planet he's been orbiting. He looks calmly up at Mrs. Bunyan as if she has politely asked him if he would like a glass of lemonade.

Yes?

"THAT'S THREE OWL POINTS!" When Leon does not look sufficiently upset by this punishment, she adds, "AND A TRIP TO THE PRINCIPAL'S OFFICE!"

Mrs. Bunyan grabs the bright red bowling pin from the bookshelf and places it not very gently on Leon's desk.

OOOOOHHhhh...

says the class in unison.

Mrs. Bunyan snaps her head around to shut us up. It works.

Everyone knows that if you're carrying a red bowling pin in the halls of Tiddlywhump Elementary, it means you have been sent to the principal's office and are supposed to go *directly* there instead of, say, stopping to take a long, relaxing drink at the water fountain.

The principal's office is pretty much the worst
thing that can happen to you at Tiddlywhump.
It's common knowledge that Principal Jones
used to be either a professional lion tamer or the
warden of a secret underground prison. She is
tall. She is tough. And awful things happen when
you get sent to see her.

Rumors

of awful happenings include:

1. Being hung upside down by your ankles
and tickled with a feather until you give up
all your darkest secrets

HAHAHAHAHAHA OKAY I DID IT!

2. Being dropped through
a trapdoor into a pool of
murky water filled with
feisty toothless eels that gnaw
endlessly on your toes

3. Being tied to a chair while Principal Jones's secretary, Mrs. Breath (rhymes with *death*), reads to you from the *P* section of the *Oxford English Dictionary*

puerile, puerilism, pue... rilities, pue...

Which is why, as much as I don't mind breaking the occasional rule in the name of justice or self-respect or problem solving, I am careful to never, ever get sent to the principal's office.

I feel sorry for Leon. He's not a bad guy. I think he's just a superweirdo who really likes to draw, really doesn't care about his teeth, and may or may not like avocados.

Apparently, Leon is still lost in outer space, because he doesn't seem in the least bit concerned about his trip to see Principal Jones. In fact, he's sort of halfway smiling as he takes his bowling pin and hall pass and disappears into the hallway.

Mrs. Bunyan continues sharing her thoughts on soft-bristled toothbrushes until she is silenced by a sudden loud buzz that makes us all jump, followed by a crackle that makes our ears hurt, followed by the unmistakable voice that always makes us worry a little.

The voice of Principal Jones.

Good morning, Owls of Tiddlywhump. It is Friday, the eighteenth of December, and it is thirty-seven degrees outside. Later this afternoon, we will be gathering for the winter assembly. I remind you all to walk quietly and respectfully in the halls on your way to the auditorium.

Principal Jones pauses for a second so that each of us has a moment to think,

Or else you will be hung upside down by your ankles or gnawed upon by toothless eels.

Principal Jones continues,
"I want to take a moment to
recognize fourth grader Emily Estevez
for contributing twenty hours of her time
to Tiddlywhump Hills Soup Kitchen this
month. Eddie thanks her for
her generous service."

I glance over at Emily, who is sitting there as if nothing out of the ordinary has happened, even though it's obvious she has just pulled into the lead in the battle for the Eddie Award. She is a formidable opponent.

Unfortunately, there is not enough time for me to do something equally amazing and admirable between now and the assembly. My only hope is that Principal Jones realizes that I, too, *would* have been at the soup kitchen . . . if only I weren't so busy saving the world in *other* equally important ways.

> Thank you, Owls. That's all for this morning,

says Principal Jones.

> I will see you this afternoon at the assembly. Have a good day, and remember to always be wise like Eddie.

Then there is another CRACKLE and another loud BUZZ!

Even though we know it's coming, it always makes us jump. I am wondering why Tiddlywhump can't get a better intercom, when Tracy Dublinger raises her hand and tells Mrs. Bunyan that she forgot to floss her teeth after breakfast this morning and that she's very worried about what might happen if she goes all day with little bits of grapefruit stuck between her molars.

> Can I please, please, please go to the nurse and get some floss?

Tracy says this as if her arm has just fallen off and she needs someone to sew it back on.

I am waiting for Mrs. Bunyan to take away one of Tracy Dublinger's Owl Points for being so ridiculous, but instead, she gets very concerned and goes over to Tracy's desk and peers directly into her mouth.

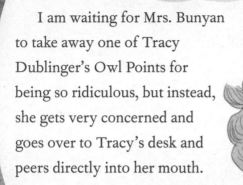

Oh dear.

Yes, this is very serious, indeed. Go see Nurse Crockett right away.

Tracy Dublinger is practically in tears as she takes her hall pass and runs out of the classroom. We hear her making panicked little whoops as she scurries down the hall toward the main office.

WHOOP!

WHOOP!

WHOOOOOP!

Even if Tracy Dublinger

kissed a slug on its slimy mouth

while eating guacamole

and riding on a unicycle,

I would not have her as a best friend.

Mrs. Bunyan looks extremely pleased with herself, as if she has just rescued an orphan from a runaway freight train.

Tammy Dublinger smiles proudly to show the world that *her* teeth are straight and spectacular and already very well flossed.

Mrs. Bunyan picks up her tooth poster again and launches into a lengthy speech about how our future happiness depends on the state of our mouths. I watch the clock as minutes pass and am wondering whether it's possible to actually die of boredom when another sudden loud **BUZZ** crackles from the intercom.

R.I.P.

MOXIE McCOY

DIED TOO YOUNG
FROM HEARING AN
ENDLESS LECTURE
ABOUT TEETH

This is highly unusual. We haven't had more than one set of announcements since Wally Belvedere sneaked his hamster Otis into school and Otis escaped in the music room, and Principal Jones came over the loudspeaker to ask everyone to please *not* squish Otis if we happened to see him.

Principal Jones starts to speak.

It seems that . . . . there aren't going to be any awards today.

Not until we get to the bottom of this. . . .

She pauses, as 163 kids lean forward and wonder to themselves what in the world Principal Jones is talking about. Later, I would realize that only 162 of us were wondering. Because one of us already knew.

CHAPTER 5: THE CRIME OF THE CENTURY

Principal Jones's voice sounds different than it usually does, a little bit sad and a little unsure, as if she's trying to figure out what to say. Which isn't like Principal Jones at all. She is usually *entirely* certain of what to say, as if she has been practicing for days. But then she continues, and suddenly it all makes perfect sense.

Someone has stolen Eddie.

He's gone.

For a second, all of us are too stunned to even breathe. And then there are a few loud

GASPS.

At first my mind is blank because I can't quite believe what I just heard. But then it hits me like a renegade asteroid slamming into a lonely moon. Someone stole Eddie. MY Eddie. OUR Eddie.

I can't help but think about Milton. I don't know if there's anyone in the world who loves Eddie more. Milton does everything he can to be like Eddie at every moment of every day and probably even when he's sleeping.

Other than not having wings or a beak or a monocle, Milton even kind of *looks* like Eddie.

Across the room, Megan Lacey is actually crying. I understand where she's coming from, but I am too mad to cry. Stealing Eddie is like punching a puppy or your own little brother. And even though I sometimes *feel* like punching Milton, or at least pinching him, I never, ever do. And I never, ever would.

DETECTIVE
CODE OF
HONOR
1. No punching.
2. No punching a puppy.
3. No pinching.
4. No pinching little brothers.
5. Never.

DON'T WORRY ABOUT ME... JUST LEARN!!

Principal Jones continues:

We're going to get to the bottom of this.

If anyone has any idea what happened to Eddie, I want you to come tell me right away. For now, get back to your work. Eddie would want us to go on learning.

We hear the crackle and buzz and jump just a little and then sit there in silence. Even Mrs. Bunyan looks a little bit lost.

But I know *exactly* what needs to be done.

There are times when it's important to follow the rules and times when it's important not to. This is one of the *important not to* times. Disaster has struck. The school is in peril, and clearly I am the only one with the courage, patience, and wisdom to set things right. Eddie needs me. Milton needs me. Tiddlywhump needs me. I will catch the crook. I will find the owl. I will **save the day.**

I start by raising my hand.

Mrs. Bunyan looks over at me with exasperation. Clearly, she was looking forward to getting back to her tooth talk.

Yes, Moxie?

I have to go to the bathroom.

I know from reading all 58 volumes of the Annabelle Adams, Girl Detective, series 37½ times that it's important to get to the scene of a crime as soon as possible, while the evidence is fresh, before the clues are swept away.

In case you are wondering, Annabelle is basically the #1 kid detective in the world. She is only 12, but she solves every problem single-handedly. I do not know why she does not use both hands. I guess she's just that good.

I pretend that I'm heading toward the bathroom, but after making sure that no one is looking, I tiptoe down the back hall by the cafeteria and through the part of the school where the kindergarten and first-grade classrooms are.

The little kids are so busy crying and asking for hugs and blowing their noses that no one is paying attention to me. As you might expect, I move undetected, like a silent shadow mixed with an invisible lion.

Which means I have no problem making it back to the lobby, where Eddie's empty case is waiting for me. It might be the saddest, loneliest, most awful thing I have ever seen in my entire life.

But, as Annabelle Adams often says,

A crime scene is not just a place where something awful has happened. It is also a place where *justice* can be found. Because, no matter how careful, every crook leaves clues.

It is my job to find them. And I have only moments to do it.

And so I survey the scene, jotting notes in my tiny blue detective notebook.

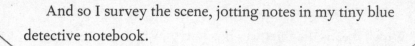

Eddie's case is surrounded by velvet ropes like the kind you see in the bank or the post office. The ropes are there to keep kids from actually touching the case. Basically, to keep Eddie safe from excitable kindergartners who want to give him a hug. This is an actual problem. Eddie is extremely lovable.

It is clear by looking at the poles that hold up the ropes that someone has recently moved them. One of them is out of place. On a normal day, the ropes are very carefully and symmetrically positioned, because Mr. Hammer is so good at his job.

So . . . whoever stole Eddie wasn't being very careful. Which means the thief was in a hurry. Which means he or she is probably *not* a professional bank robber. This is an important piece of information, and I write it down.

There, on the case itself, I see another clue, a greasy thumbprint, right next to the knob you would use to open the case.

I know the thumbprint must belong to the thief because I remember seeing Mr. Hammer cleaning the glass just this morning.

I make a sketch of the door and the location of the thumbprint. This will be critical evidence if the case ever goes before a skeptical jury.

But I am looking for a third and final clue. In my experience, it is extremely difficult to solve mysteries without at least three clues, because, as Annabelle Adams proves in Volume 3: *Third Time's the Charm*—in which three banks are robbed simultaneously by three bandits (who are actually triplets) and she apprehends all three in the span of three hours at the request of Glenwood Perkins III—each crook makes at least three mistakes.

I look around for anything that stands out. But there is nothing. Everything else is completely ordinary.

I hear the familiar whistling of my favorite custodian as he comes down the hallway. I shove my hands in my pockets to look casual and wait for Mr. Hammer to turn the corner.

"Hey, Slim."

"Hey, Marvin. I am looking for clues," I say before he has a chance to ask why I'm not in class.

"What sorts of clues?"

"Anything that will help me figure out who stole Eddie. Do you know that he's missing?"

"I do," says Mr. Hammer. "I certainly do."

"When was the last time you saw him?"

"Right after school started. I was walking down to the art room and saw Eddie in his case."

"Did you give a friendly wave?" It's what I would have done.

Mr. Hammer smiles. "I certainly did. As I came back up the hallway a few minutes later, I thought I heard footsteps. But when I turned the corner, no one was there. And the case was empty."

So Mr. Hammer was the first one at the scene of the crime! This is important information. I am tempted to gasp. But detectives do not gasp. And so I say "I see," which is something that Annabelle Adams says constantly. She must have excellent eyesight.

Was there anything around the case? *Blood*, maybe?

All I found was this,

he says, reaching into his pocket and pulling out a bright green hall pass.

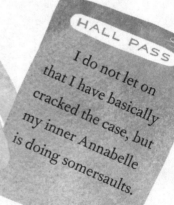

HALL PASS

I do not let on that I have basically cracked the case, but my inner Annabelle is doing somersaults.

I take the hall pass, trying to pretend that it's no big deal. But I know right away that this could be the third clue!

"I *see*," I say. "Where did you find it, if I may ask?"

"Right under the case," says Mr. Hammer. "Just the tip of it was poking out."

67

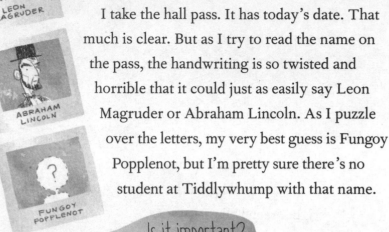

LEON
MAGRUDER

ABRAHAM
LINCOLN

FUNGOY
POPPLENOT

I take the hall pass. It has today's date. That much is clear. But as I try to read the name on the pass, the handwriting is so twisted and horrible that it could just as easily say Leon Magruder or Abraham Lincoln. As I puzzle over the letters, my very best guess is Fungoy Popplenot, but I'm pretty sure there's no student at Tiddlywhump with that name.

Is it important? Mr. Hammer asks.

Possibly, but it's far too early to tell. Thank you, Marvin.

No problem. Good luck, Slim.

Marvin . . . before you go, I just have to ask . . . can you ride a unicycle—either with or without your eyes closed?

Mr. Hammer is so darn nice that I decide to give him another chance. I might be able to overlook his feelings about slugs if he turns out to have remarkable balance.

Never tried.

But I'm guessing the answer is no.

68

I am disappointed, of course, but only a little, because today I am a one-person wrecking ball of problem-solving fury. I can't let missing Maude make me lose my edge. My search for a new best friend can wait until the crisis has passed.

I give Marvin a little nod, and he gives me a little nod and then pushes his handy rolling mop bucket back down the hallway.

He does not seem to notice or care that I still have the hall pass, and so I decide not to tell him that it might be the single most important piece of paper in the history of Tiddlywhump Elementary.

I am taking a final look at Eddie's case when I hear more footsteps coming down the side hall toward the lobby.

I have just enough time to stuff the hall pass in my pocket and put on my most innocent face before Principal Jones comes around the corner and almost knocks me over with her

LONG, DARK STARE.

"Moxie McCoy," she says.

I am tempted to remind her that people call me Slim, but it doesn't seem like exactly the right moment.

"Principal Jones," I say, trying to be very relaxed and normal sounding.

"Why aren't you in class?" she asks, not super suspiciously but not super *not* suspiciously, either.

It is a reasonable question, but one I am not prepared to answer.

I . . . dropped my pencil,

I say, holding up my pencil and realizing as I do that, as an excuse for being absent from class, it doesn't quite hold up.

"Do you have a hall pass?" she asks. At Tiddlywhump Elementary, being in the hallway without a hall pass is like being in outer space without an oxygen tank.

"Of course," I say, handing her my hall pass—before realizing that it is the one Mr. Hammer found under Eddie's case *and not the one that Mrs. Bunyan wrote for me*!

As Principal Jones squints at the hall pass, I consider whether it's better to run for it or play dead. Getting caught with *someone else's* hall pass would probably earn me a trip to the eel tank. Luckily, however, Principal Jones doesn't seem to be having any more luck than I did figuring out whose name is written on it.

"Does Mrs. Bunyan teach you penmanship?" she asks.

"Of course not!" I say. Penmanship is for first and second graders. You would think Principal Jones would know this.

She nods and hands the hall pass back to me, apparently unable to prove that it isn't mine.

I'm assuming you're on your way back to your classroom at this very moment?

Absolutely.

Before you go, I just have to ask: Do you have any idea who took Eddie?

It's just a simple question, but the way she says it makes me feel like all the bones in my body have suddenly turned into cottage cheese.

I understand why she is asking. As I learned from

Annabelle Adams, Girl Detective

Volume 46:
Again and Again and Again,

sometimes criminals return to the scene of their crime to rub their hands together and cackle maniacally while enjoying all the trouble they have caused.

But I am not a criminal.

Principal Jones, I say, as deadly serious as I've ever said anything in my entire life,

I do not know who stole Eddie. I consider the theft of Eddie a *serious crime*—not only against our school but against the ideals of courage, patience, and wisdom for which Eddie stands.

Principal Jones looks at me as if I've just sprouted an extra eyeball. Then her gaze softens a little, and I can tell she believes me.

All right,

she says.

I hope you understand that I had to ask. You can take your pencil and head back to class.

She starts to turn, but I stop her with my words.

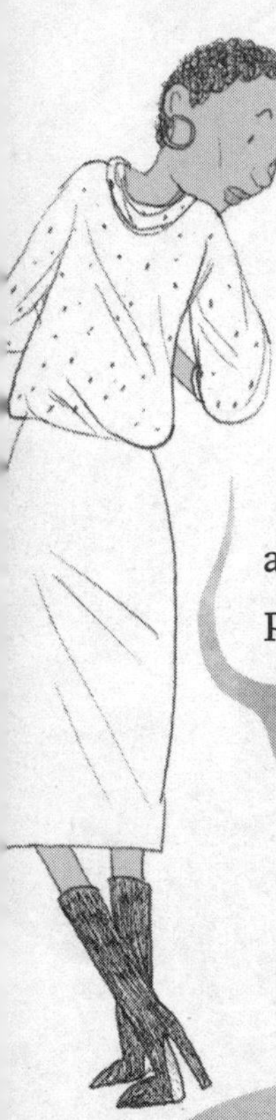

One
more
thing.

I can tell she's surprised that I've spoken again. People don't usually say anything to Principal Jones until they are invited to do so.

Yes? she says. Her voice is not entirely friendly, but I am feeling rather brave.

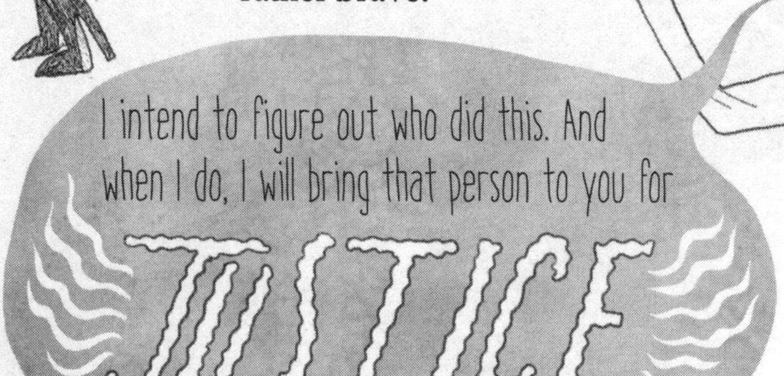

I intend to figure out who did this. And when I do, I will bring that person to you for

JUSTICE

I say "justice" in a sinister whisper to let her know that I mean business.

74

Principal Jones gives me a little nod, which basically means, *I believe in you, Moxie McCoy, and I know you can do this. Tiddlywhump Elementary is lucky to have a student as courageous, patient, and wise as you who also has an insect named after her.*

Then she turns and heads back to her office. Probably to tell Mrs. Breath to read to Leon from the *Oxford English Dictionary* until he tells her what planet he was on.

POCOCURANTE POCOCURANTE

As I walk back down the hall to Mrs. Bunyan's classroom, I'm struck by a realization so powerful it makes me nearly two inches taller. As sad as I am that Eddie has been stolen, this is also my golden opportunity to prove to Principal Jones that I'm even more amazing than the amazing Emily Estevez.

Finding our missing owl is going to take every ounce of courage, patience, and wisdom I can muster. But if I can pull it off, the Eddie Award will be mine.

CHAPTER 6: THE SUSPECTS

When I get back to class, Bob, Leon, and Tracy are at their desks, and everyone is working on piñatas for

THE WINTER CARNIVAL,

the big open house that happens right after winter break. Our parents come to school and look at our artwork and eat gingersnaps and listen as we sing cheerful, winter-themed songs.

The piñatas are supposed to say something about "who we are." It's exactly the sort of ridiculous assignment that only Mrs. Bunyan could think up.

Leon, who seems to have survived his encounter with Principal Jones, has created a one-armed, three-eyed superhero. Bob built a lopsided hamburger with way too many toppings. Emily's piñata is in the shape of planet Earth.

Because it is our home, she said when Mrs. Bunyan made us go around and explain why we had chosen whatever it was we had chosen.

Tammy Dublinger's piñata looks like Tammy Dublinger, although she says it's supposed to be Tracy Dublinger.

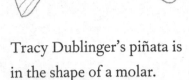

Tracy Dublinger's piñata is in the shape of a molar.

I, of course, am working on a large-scale replica of the *Moximaxus*, complete with proboscis. Even though papier-mâché does not do it justice, my piñata is extremely intimidating. I don't know how playing with balloons and wet newspaper is supposed to prepare us for the future, but it's way more fun than converting fractions to decimals, which is what we'd otherwise be doing right about now.

As I sit down at my desk, Tracy Dublinger is showing her molar piñata to Mrs. Bunyan, who is admiring it and making all sorts of ridiculous happy sounds.

I have a dentist appointment this afternoon, and I'd really like to take it to show my hygienist, says Tracy.

But it's so beautiful! says Mrs. Bunyan.

We *must* have it here for the Winter Carnival!

I'll definitely bring it back after.

Well, all right, then, says Mrs. Bunyan, laughing as if someone has said something really funny.

I half expect Tracy and Mrs. Bunyan to do a high five or start braiding each other's hair.

78

I try to slide back into my seat while Mrs. Bunyan is distracted by all this tooth-related excitement. But Bob Tuttleman sees me and says,

HI, MOXIE,

a lot too loud, and suddenly Mrs. Bunyan notices that I'm back.

I like Bob, but if you put him in a room with an alligator and told him not to touch the alligator, the first thing he would do is give it a hug.

"And where have *you* been?" says Mrs. Bunyan. I remind her that I have been in the bathroom.

"*All* this time?" she says.

I look at the clock. I've been gone for 20 minutes. I'm trying to come up with a really good explanation for why it took so long, when Mrs. Bunyan takes matters into her own hands.

"That's an Owl Point!" she shouts, taking out her secret teacher notebook. Tracy gives me a satisfied smirk, and Bob giggles the way he always does when anyone loses an Owl Point. If I cared one hoot about the Golden Owl, it might sting a little. But I don't, and so it doesn't.

I walk across the room and pick up my *Moximaxus* piñata. It's not until I start painting its savage papier-mâché pincers a terrifying shade of green that I realize the true importance of the hall pass Mr. Hammer found by Eddie's case.

Every grade has its own color of hall pass, and green is the color for fourth grade. And the hall pass that Mr. Hammer found—the one that was surely dropped by the thief—is green!

Suddenly, instead of 163 suspects, there are only 23, because that's how many fourth graders not named Moxie McCoy are at Tiddlywhump Elementary.

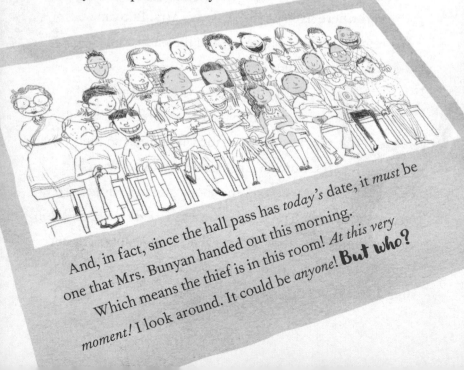

And, in fact, since the hall pass has *today's* date, it *must* be one that Mrs. Bunyan handed out this morning. Which means the thief is in this room! *At this very moment!* I look around. It could be *anyone!* **But who?**

It could be Bob Tuttleman. He asked to go to the bathroom. He would have had plenty of time to take Eddie, but if Bob stole our beloved mascot, where is Eddie now?

Or Leon! Maybe he acted weird on purpose so he could get out of class and steal Eddie! But he couldn't have taken Eddie with him to Principal Jones's office, could he?

And what about Tracy Dublinger? She went to the nurse's office after discovering her flossing crisis. Maybe on the way she took a detour through the front lobby. But she had seemed so *genuinely* concerned about the state of her gums. And what could Tracy possibly want with Eddie?

And then . . . the *fourth* suspect, which I consider a long shot, but a detective must consider *every* possibility . . .

Emily Estevez, who came in late and picked up a hall pass at the front office. She told Mrs. Bunyan she had *lost* her pass, but . . . maybe she actually *dropped* it in the middle of stealing Eddie!

But why in the world would the good and perfect and kind and thoughtful Emily Estevez risk her Eddie Award front-runner status with such a reckless act on today of all days?

None of it makes sense. And yet one of these four *must* have paid a visit to Eddie's case this morning. One of them *must* be the culprit.

PRIME
SUSPECTS

1. BOB

2. LEON

3. TRACY

4. EMILY

It's a genuine mystery. But as Annabelle Adams always says,

> A mystery is nothing but a solution that is waiting to be found.

I look around the room for some sort of sign, *anything* that will point me in the right direction.

In

Volume 28:

A Nose for Fear,

Annabelle says she can smell a frightened criminal the minute she walks into a room—though she never describes what that smell *is*, exactly.

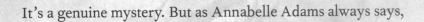

If I had to guess, I'd assume that the fear of a crook smells something like bacon, but I do not smell bacon at the moment.

Tracy smiles wickedly at her enormous molar, which is, admittedly, fantastic. It is perfectly shaped and so smooth that it practically gleams. Again, however, wicked smiling is pretty much an everyday affair for Tracy Dublinger.

Bob looks as if he'd really like to eat his gigantic hamburger piñata, which is pretty much what you'd expect from Bob on an average day.

And Emily is painting the Pacific Ocean while smiling at her papier-mâché Earth with exactly the sort of love and respect that you would expect from her fantastic and extraordinary self.

Instead of painting his piñata, Leon is drawing comics on the side of it, though much more quietly than before. This is a little unexpected, but given what he's just been through with the eels, it's completely understandable.

None of them look like criminal masterminds— but one of them *must* be. The answer is right in front of me, but *I do not see it*.

I suddenly miss Maude so much that it hurts like a pinch deep inside me.

I open my notebook and look at the sketch of her I made in the middle of the night.

There she is with her three dimples

and her kind smile.

One by one, I read through my list of questions, each of which reminds me of why I love her so much and why I will never find a friend like her again.

If Maude were here, she'd know what to do with these clues. She'd know the right questions to ask next.

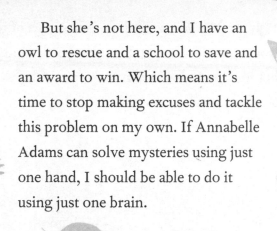

But she's not here, and I have an owl to rescue and a school to save and an award to win. Which means it's time to stop making excuses and tackle this problem on my own. If Annabelle Adams can solve mysteries using just one hand, I should be able to do it using just one brain.

The bell rings for recess.

Mrs. Bunyan tells us to bring our piñatas outside so the paint can dry.

I stash my *Moximaxus* in the sunniest part of the playground and look around for a suspect to interrogate. But before I see Bob or Leon or Emily or the Dublingers, someone else catches my eye.

It's Milton. And he doesn't look good.

Whenever he's confused or angry or trying to figure something out, Milton stands at the far end of the schoolyard and stares at the factory across the river. He calls it his thinking place. I have no idea why it's a better place to think than anywhere else.

Remembering my promise to Mom, I walk over to see how he's doing.

"Don't worry," I say. "I'll get Eddie back. I found some clues."

Milton doesn't say anything and doesn't even look at me, but I can tell that he is listening. And I can tell he's thinking, because he is pulling on his right earlobe, which is something he does whenever his gears are turning.

To make him feel better, I tell him about the thumbprint and the fourth-grade hall pass. This seems to get his attention.

"Was anything out of the ordinary?" he asks.

"The poles that hold up the ropes around Eddie's case were a little crooked."

"Hmm . . . What side of the knob was the thumbprint on?"

I look at my drawing. "On the left," I say. "Why do you ask?"

"Every detail can be important."

He's right about that. Annabelle Adams ranks paying attention to details right below maintaining clean fingernails and never chewing bubble gum while talking to a diplomat on her top secret list of detective tips.

But why? asks Milton, miserable as a cat in a bath.

The thief's hands must have been greasy, I say, assuming he's still thinking about the thumbprint.

No—why would someone want to take Eddie?

It's an excellent question. Annabelle would be the first to point out that the key to finding Eddie might be figuring out who had the most to gain from owl theft. That person would have had a *motive to commit the crime*.

"I intend to find out," I say, though it doesn't seem to cheer him up. I look at my watch. Precious minutes of recess are ticking away. "I need to talk to the suspects. Are you going to be all right?"

Milton says nothing and does not look at me. He just pulls on his earlobe and stares out across the river.

I leave him there and head back across the school yard, more convinced than ever before that this strange little person cannot be my actual brother.

Without even trying, I spot Bob Tuttleman. It's impossible to miss him. He is extremely busy smiling near the swing set.

Hey, Bob. I'm trying to remember the last time I saw Bob in a bad mood.

Hey, he says cheerfully. It's hard to imagine that I'm looking at a criminal.

How did it go in the bathroom earlier?

I ask, trying to keep things casual.

I immediately realize the question is pretty personal, and Bob's face lets me know he thinks so, too. But I can also tell that Bob is pretty much afraid of me and is worried what I might do to him if he doesn't talk.

Well...? I ask.

Um... pretty good.

I'm going to ask you a few questions now, Bob.

Okay, he says, though I can tell he thinks it's not okay at all.

What's the opposite of down? Up!

 What's two plus two? Four?

 What's the capital of Texas? Um...Dallas?

 Is soup delicious? Wait...was I right about Dallas?

 Doesn't matter, Bob. IS SOUP DELICIOUS? Yeah.

 Wrong. How about avocados? Yuck.

You're not doing very well, Bob. Next question: Did you steal Eddie this morning on your way to the bathroom?

Of course not! *Never!*

Bob looks deeply wounded, as if I've just ripped the ear off his teddy bear. But that was *exactly* my intention.

 ow.

Annabelle Adams will often try to rattle her suspects to see if she can get under their skin and make them do something foolish.

In

VOLUME 19:
IN YOUR FACE,

Annabelle's relentless questioning annoys a thieving taxi driver so completely that, at the end of a 20-minute ride, he hands her the keys to his cab, admits to stealing the mayor's crystal punch bowl, and literally begs to be put in handcuffs.

I think I've pushed Bob just far enough for the time being. But I will keep my eye on him. Now that he's spooked, what he does next might be the most important clue of all. What he does next is move to the other side of the swing set and start smiling with enthusiasm over there.

I continue to watch Bob out of the corner of my eye as I go find Tammy and Tracy, who are playing tetherball.

Hello, various Dublingers.

Hello, *Moxie,* says one of them, pronouncing my name like it is some kind of insult. I am ever so slightly offended but refuse to show it. I am working, and so I must be professional.

Pretty lame about Eddie. Don't you guys think?

The only lame thing is that you haven't caught the crook yet.

Yeah. What kind of detective are you?

I take a deep breath. Being professional
with the Dublingers is like being professional
with a two-headed sea monster.

> I just wonder if Tracy saw anything *out of
> the ordinary* when she was on her way to
> the nurse's office to get her dental floss?

One of the Dublingers whips her head
toward me, and I know it must be Tracy. I've
touched a nerve. This is good.

"I don't know how you think I could have
noticed *anything* about *anything*," she says,
like an actress in a really bad TV show. "I
was in *genuine distress*!" With that, she hits
the tetherball so hard it nearly
takes her sister's head off.

"*Hey!*" snaps Tammy.

Tracy says nothing. She is staring
at me the way a wood chipper might look at
a log.

Clearly, I'm not going to get anything else out of the Dublingers for now, and I have absolutely no interest in asking their opinion of soup, so I look for Leon. I find him sitting on the cold pavement next to his piñata. He is drawing, of course.

Hey, Leon, I say.

Leon says nothing.

Hey, LEON.

Still nothing. He doesn't even flinch. I wonder if Leon is deaf. It's entirely possible. Or it could just be an act.

I have to say, Leon just doesn't *seem* like a criminal. He seems like a crazy, half-deaf kid who really likes to draw.

But I have to be sure.

HEY, LEON!

Leon looks up. "Yeah?" he says, as if I've just tapped him on the shoulder and handed him a cookie.

"What happened this morning in the principal's office?" I ask, pretending to be very concerned about his well-being. "Are you okay?"

"I'm great," he says, smiling like a puppy that has just been scratched behind the ear.

"Seriously?" I ask. I lean in and quietly add,

Did you get hung upside down by your ankles?

Leon laughs and says, "No way. Principal Jones is really nice."

That's when I realize that Leon has been completely *brainwashed*. Maybe after Mrs. Breath reads to you from the *Oxford English Dictionary* until you confess your crimes and secrets, she reprograms your brain so that you forget the entire thing. It makes perfect sense.

Which means that Leon might have stolen Eddie **and now hAS** NO MEMORY OF IT. This is a very complicated possibility.

In Volume 8: *Cry If You Want To*, Annabelle encounters a brainwashed butler who is the only one who knows which of FIVE birthday cakes belonging to the governor's quintuplet daughters is going to EXPLODE.

To get the information she needs without ruining the four perfectly good cakes, Annabelle has to unbrainwash him by playing his favorite childhood lullaby on the Flügelhorn.

(His mother was a famous flügelhorn player.)

But I do not have a flügelhorn. And I do not know Leon's favorite childhood lullaby. And as far as I know, there is no danger of a birthday cake exploding today.

I'll have to study up on other strategies for unbrainwashing people. But for the time being, Leon is obviously a DEAD END.

Carry on, Leon,

I say.

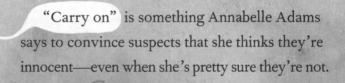

"Carry on" is something Annabelle Adams says to convince suspects that she thinks they're innocent—even when she's pretty sure they're not.

PRIME SUSPECTS

✓ 1. BOB
✓ 2. LEON
✓ 3. TRACY
4. EMILY

I have one more suspect to question, and I don't have to look very hard to find her.

For whatever reason, Emily Estevez is lying on a bench with her eyes closed. Maybe she is preparing her Eddie Award acceptance speech. Or perhaps she's hoping that pretending to be asleep will keep me from asking her hard-hitting questions.

Good day, Emily. Emily says nothing.

In fact, she seems to be SNORING.

I lean in. The SNORE is very convincing.

I conclude it must be a really good fake

SNORE

No one sleeps on a bench during recess in December. This is not napping weather.

I give Emily a nudge with my knee. She groans a little. I give her another nudge. She groans a little more.

I decide to hurry things along a bit.

The elephant is ON FIRE!

Emily's eyes fly open, and she sits up suddenly.

Oh no!

she says.

What elephant?

Is it hurt?

Where am I?

There is no elephant, I say.

And it's not on fire. You're on a bench.

Thank goodness, says Emily.

She looks relieved. Even when pretending to be asleep on a cold bench, Emily Estevez is bighearted. It's half galling and half inspiring. Again, I am reminded that she is just the kind of person I might like to be friends with if not for the fact that she is on the verge of stealing my Eddie Award and might just be an owl thief.

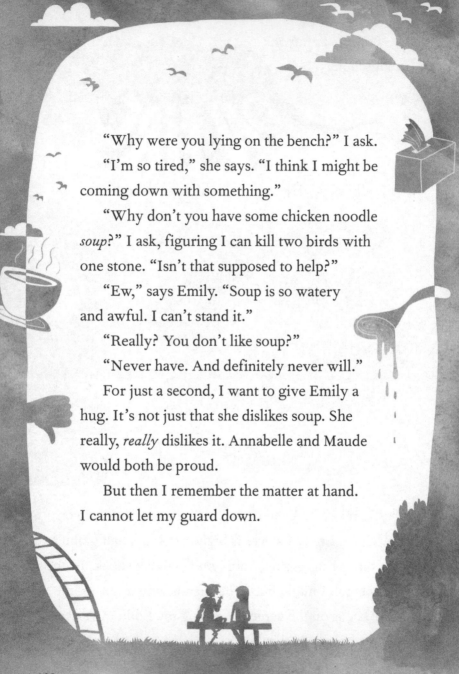

"Why were you lying on the bench?" I ask.

"I'm so tired," she says. "I think I might be coming down with something."

"Why don't you have some chicken noodle *soup*?" I ask, figuring I can kill two birds with one stone. "Isn't that supposed to help?"

"Ew," says Emily. "Soup is so watery and awful. I can't stand it."

"Really? You don't like soup?"

"Never have. And definitely never will."

For just a second, I want to give Emily a hug. It's not just that she dislikes soup. She really, *really* dislikes it. Annabelle and Maude would both be proud.

But then I remember the matter at hand. I cannot let my guard down.

"You haven't seen anything . . . *out of the ordinary* today, have you?" I ask.

"I don't think so," says Emily. "Why do you ask?"

"I ask because you came through the lobby this morning right around the time that Eddie was being stolen."

"Yes, Eddie was still there in his case when I walked by."

"Is that so . . . ?" I say, as if I'm not convinced at all that it is.

"Cross my heart and hope to die," says Emily.

And she says it so earnestly that it seems impossible that she could be telling anything but the 100% truth. I'm trying to come up with another hard-hitting detective question when Emily beats me to the punch.

I know what question I'd be asking.

And what is that?

"Why is January?"

I consider scratching my head, because that's what Annabelle Adams always does when she comes across a situation that confuses her, but my head does not itch, and I don't want to waste a single moment that could be spent getting to the bottom of things.

"What do you mean by that, exactly?"

Emily smiles. "Whenever I reach a dead end and can't figure something out, I ask myself 'Why is January?' or some other question like it. Such as

"When is happiness?" or

"Which is yesterday?" or

"How is asparagus?"

"But those questions don't have answers," I say. Maybe Emily isn't quite as smart as I thought.

"That's the whole point," she says. "Because when you try to answer them anyway, your brain has to wander around. And then it gets unstuck so that it's easier to solve the original problem. But . . ."

"Yes?"

"It works best when you talk it through with someone else. Whenever I ask 'Why is January?' in my own head, I just end up getting lost. Want to try?"

"Why not?" I decide to humor Emily, even though I am pretty sure that any problem-solving technique worth its salt would appear somewhere in the 58 volumes of Annabelle Adams, Girl Detective.

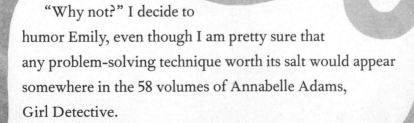

So . . . what's the problem we're trying to solve?

WHO TOOK EDDIE?

I thought I had already made this quite clear.

Okay, good. So . . . Slim. People call you *Slim*, right?

Always.

Okay, Slim. *Why* is January?

What does that have to do with—

Stop.

You're missing the point. Just try to actually answer the question.

WHY IS JANUARY?

I think about it for a second. I have no idea.
January is just . . . January. It always has been
and it always will be.

"I have no idea."

"Me neither. So maybe let's try a related
question: Why is January *called* January?"

"Well, it has to be called *something*."

"Why didn't they call it Jennifer?"

"Because that would be ridiculous!"

"But why *January*?"

Because January is
the *first* month.

I hear a voice
behind me.

It's Milton. I swear he moves so silently he would make an excellent ninja if only he were a better leaper.

"Hi, Milton," says Emily.

"What are you doing here?" I ask. I know I'm supposed to be nice to him, but I wish he wouldn't bother me while I'm working.

Milton ignores my question.

January is named after Janus, the Roman god of doors and beginnings, which is why the first month of the year is named after him.

I did not know that, says Emily.

I did, I say, as convincingly as I can.

I want Milton to go back to his thinking place, but before I can tell him to do so, Emily continues.

"Is your brain unstuck?"

"I think so," I say. I'm not sure whether it is or not, but I certainly don't want to admit it.

"Good! So now let's go back to the original question. Who took Eddie?"

Right. The original question. The problem at hand. The missing owl. I think through the evidence again. The hall pass. The out-of-place ropes. The greasy thumbprint.

Bob.

Leon.

Tracy.

Emily.

"I'm still not sure," I say.

Milton says nothing. He is tugging on his earlobe.

Emily shrugs. "It doesn't always work the first time."

The bell rings, interrupting my thoughts and delighting Mrs. Bunyan, who sees every minute of recess as a minute she can't spend making us sit still at our desks.

"Let's go get our piñatas," says Emily.

I am admiring my *Moximaxus*, when Mrs. Bunyan comes by and decides our piñatas are not quite dry and that we should leave them out until second recess.

As I get back in line, I glimpse the various suspects. Tammy and Tracy seem to have made up and are using their MIND POWERS to prepare for the spelling test.

Leon now seems to be drawing on his hand.

Emily is using her arm for a pillow as she leans against the cold brick wall. I think she might be asleep again.

And Bob is . . . chewing?

Yes, his mouth is definitely full of something, and he's trying to chew slowly enough that Mrs. Bunyan doesn't notice. With good reason. Food is completely forbidden during recess.

I think about Janus as I watch Bob chewing and chewing and chewing.

January is the FIRST month.

WHICH is WHY it is named after the god of BEGINNINGS

Makes perfect sense.

Bob finally swallows whatever it is, and then he reaches into his coat pocket and comes back with . . . a doughnut hole, which he pops into his mouth before licking the sugar off his fingers.

And then my suddenly unstuck mind puts it all together. I want to say

EUREKA!

but decide it's probably better just to think it.

Bob Tuttleman spent the morning eating forbidden doughnuts, _UNDER IS WHY_ he left a greasy thumb-print when he stole an owl from a glass case !!!

GOTCHA!

And just like that, the mystery is solved.

I wonder whether Bob will be sent to regular jail or to an island fortress with no windows.

Milton is way over on the other side of the school yard in the first-grade line. I'd go over and tell him the exciting news, but I don't want to get him in trouble. Not this close to his winning the Golden Owl Award.

I feel a little bit bad for Emily Estevez as she leans against the wall, fast asleep and completely unaware that she has just handed me the big break I need to take the Eddie Award away from her.

CHAPTER 7: PRINCIPAL JONES

Now that I know who took Eddie, I need to get this information to the one person who can do something about it. In Volume 24: *And Eat It, Too*, Annabelle basically solves the mystery in the first chapter—it was *the king himself* who stole the crown jewels—but before she can get the evidence to the vice-chancellor, she gets locked in the hold of a

rickety schooner taking the long route around the Cape of Good Hope—

and has to spend the next 17 chapters plotting her escape from the clutches of Dr. Fungo and his band of renegade accountants . . .

a thing she manages to do just moments before the king, by this time completely off his rocker, threatens to invade Scotland using an enormous robotic lobster.

Which is why I need to make sure Principal Jones knows as soon as possible that Bob Tuttleman could, at any moment, commit some even more horrible crime.

And so, when the class files into the building and back toward the fourth-grade classroom, I take a detour.

I am delighted to have such an excellent reason not to go back to class, because it is time for the spelling test, and I enjoy spelling tests about as much as I enjoy petting rattlesnakes.

Ophidiophobia

I admit that I am not the world's best speller, but Dad has told me over and over that some of the most intelligent people in history were terrible spellers. Which is to say, my spelling woes might be the very reason I am so good at everything else.

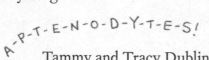

A-P-T-E-N-O-D-Y-T-E-S!   G-E-L-I-D!

Tammy and Tracy Dublinger love spelling tests more than penguins love ice. This is because they are, perhaps, the world's *best* spellers. But who has time to care about spelling when a dastardly owl thief is on the loose?

I happen to know that Principal Jones always stands outside her office after recess, watching the kindergartners and first graders and second graders as they walk back into their classrooms. My guess is that she's trying to decide which one of them to eat for lunch.

I turn the corner and see her standing there and pause for just a second. Principal Jones is the sort of person who does not want to be bothered except for when you have very important news, such as you just discovered an iguana in your lunch box. But since finding out who stole Eddie is perhaps the most important news Principal Jones will ever hear in her entire life, I take a deep breath and boldly tap her on the arm and say in my most official detective whisper,

EE EE EE EE EE K!

I know who took Eddie.

Principal Jones looks at me as if I'm a fly that just landed on her sandwich. She bends down a bit to hear me better.

Excuse me?

Clearly, this is her way of letting me know that she would rather have this conversation in private and not in front of the little kids. Which makes perfect sense. Principal Jones is also a professional.

I have important information that I would prefer to discuss in your office.

Principal Jones can tell from the expression on my face how very serious I am, because she gives me a dignified nod and leads me into the main office and then into her private office, which is in the back corner.

Principal Jones is so important that her office is actually two rooms.

First there's a waiting area where Mrs. Breath sits at her desk, daring you not to burst into tears.

Right across from the desk is a little bench where kids who have been sent to see Principal Jones have to wait while Mrs. Breath slowly devours them with her mind.

I do not like to be mean, and so I won't be mean, but I will say in completely objective terms that if there ever was a person who looks like a bulldog in a pantsuit, it is Mrs. Breath.

Fortunately, I do not have to sit on the bench. I am an invited guest of Principal Jones.

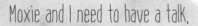

Moxie and I need to have a talk, says Principal Jones.

Please see that we are not disturbed.

Mrs. Breath gives me a mean sort of look, as if she is certain I have done some horrible thing and am about to suffer the consequences.

Principal Jones leads me into her actual office, which contains a bigger desk and a bigger bench. She gestures for me to sit down.

I look all around for the machine that hangs you by your ankles and the lever that opens up the trapdoor above the eel tank, but I don't see either. I wonder if maybe she keeps them in the closet.

You were about to tell me something.

As I prepare to deliver the exciting news, I wonder if Principal Jones might decide to just give me the Eddie Award now and tell the other kids about it later at the assembly.

"I have figured out who stole Eddie," I say. I try to say it with a flourish, as Annabelle Adams does, but it occurs to me that I do not know how a "flourish" is supposed to sound. And so I say it kind of slowly, emphasizing certain syllables.

"Excuse me?" says Principal Jones. "I have figured out who stole Eddie," I repeat, with less of a flourish this time.

Instead of clapping her hands in delight and offering me some candy from the bowl on her desk, Principal Jones looks as if she doesn't quite believe me.

"Is that so?" she says.

"Yes!" I say. I am terribly excited and wish that Dud Boggs were here to document the moment.

I wonder if the story in the *Monthly Owl* will include a picture of me getting my Eddie Award and whether there will also be a big photo of Bob Tuttleman getting carted off to jail. My mind is racing. Are there enormous cash prizes for apprehending owl thieves? Will there be a parade in my honor?

"Are you going to tell me who it is?" asks Principal Jones.

I lean closer to Principal Jones and whisper. Anyone could be listening, after all.

BOB TUTTLEMAN

Oh?

And what makes you think Bob took Eddie?

I consider it strange that Principal Jones is not more surprised. Maybe she has always suspected that Bob is owl thief material.

I explain how Bob had asked to
go to the bathroom, and I show
her the hall pass from the crime
scene (deciding not to mention
Mr. Hammer so that he doesn't
get in trouble for giving it to me).

Principal Jones squints over her glasses.

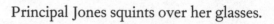

I'm pretty sure this hall pass belongs
to someone named Fungoy Popplenot.

I'm suddenly concerned that Principal Jones will
recognize the hall pass as the same one I showed her earlier,
so I decide to move on to the *other* evidence, mentioning that
the ropes around Eddie's case had
been knocked out of place, and
noting that only someone
with Bob's endless
enthusiasm would have
left such an obvious
clue while committing
such a horrible crime.

Finally, I mention the  and how Bob had been eating the doughnut holes during recess.

It's an ironclad case, I say.

Ironclad means "absolutely, 100% true," if you're not familiar with the term.

I am familiar with the term.

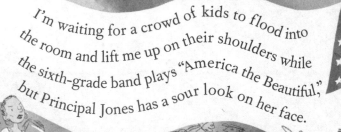

I'm waiting for a crowd of kids to flood into the room and lift me up on their shoulders while the sixth-grade band plays "America the Beautiful," but Principal Jones has a sour look on her face.

I'm afraid you're missing one important fact.

What is that? I ask, panicking at first and then getting sort of excited. Maybe Principal Jones found *another* clue that proves that Bob is also guilty of several *other* awful crimes?

"Not long after Bob left your classroom, he tripped over Mrs. Flicker's art tray and spilled paint all over the hallway. He spent the next twenty minutes helping her clean it up. Which means he couldn't have stolen Eddie."

I'm disappointed, of course. All the evidence had pointed straight to Bob.

But even Annabelle Adams doesn't always get it right on the first try.

In Volume 35:

It Is, Alas, the Real McCoy,

she accuses Professor Hardlystrong of hiding the duchess's stolen heirloom chocolate-chip-cookie recipe in his wooden leg only to discover the hard way (trying to remove the leg by vigorous yanking in the middle of a crowded ballroom) that the leg is real and that the *actual* villain is the duchess herself, who has been fooling her guests all along by serving

STORE-BOUGHT COOKIES

at her fabulous parties.

Annabelle is then forced to apologize, a thing she likes even less than being stung by bees.

"I want you to understand that accusing another student of something he did not do is a very serious thing," says Principal Jones.

"Of course," I say, "but so you know, I wasn't *accusing* Bob. I was just trying to rule him out as a suspect. An important part of solving a case is figuring out who did *not* commit the crime."

"I see . . ." says Principal Jones. She looks as if she is trying very hard not to smile, which surprises me, because usually she is so good at not smiling.

Then her face gets very serious again. "Remember that you must have *all* the facts to solve a case. And clearly you did not have all the facts."

BEEP! BEEP!

At that moment, Principal Jones's phone makes a beeping sound, and the awful voice of Mrs. Breath fills the room.

Marvin Hammer to see you.

Principal Jones presses a button on her phone. "I'll be right out," she says. "If you will excuse me for a moment," she says to me.

Principal Jones leaves, but she doesn't quite shut the door the whole way, which means I can hear Mr. Hammer when he says,

Just like you asked, I took another look around Eddie's case. And I found this underneath it.

When is the last time you cleaned under the case?

I hear Principal Jones ask.

Just this morning,

says Mr. Hammer.

Thank you, Marvin,

says Principal Jones.

That's extremely helpful.

My pleasure,

says Mr. Hammer.

Mr. Hammer has discovered *another* clue! And whatever it is found its way under Eddie's case since this morning. Which means it's almost definitely 100% likely to have something to do with the crime. Which means I *have* to figure out what it is.

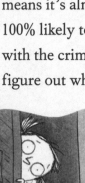

A moment later, Principal Jones returns, and part of me regrets I did not take advantage of the opportunity to peek inside her closet.

As Principal Jones sits down, she puts a pencil on her desk. I sneak a quick glance.

The pencil is purple.

It is covered with bite marks from eraser to tip.

I know exactly who it belongs to. . . .

I try to figure out where I'm going to put my Eddie Award. There is the shelf above my dresser. Or the table next to my bed. But it might look best on the mantel over the fireplace in the living room.

What was I saying . . . ?

says Principal Jones.

"You were saying something about needing *all* the facts to solve a case."

"Yes. I know you care about Eddie, and so I'm not going to punish you for accusing Bob of something he did not do, but I urge you not to jump to any more conclusions."

Of course, Principal Jones, I say.

Jumping to conclusions is the kind of thing I'd never do in 1,000 years.

I already know that the crook is Tracy Dublinger, who *always* writes with purple pencils.

For some
reason, she thinks
this makes her better than
those of us who write with regular old
yellow pencils. Even Tammy Dublinger uses yellow
pencils. For a while, she tried to use the same color pencil as
Tracy, but Tracy kept switching colors. First Tracy would
use red, and then Tammy would use red. Then Tracy would
use blue, so Tammy would use blue. Finally, when Tracy
switched to purple, Tammy gave up and went
back to plain, regular old yellow, just
like the rest of us.

Which means that
any purple pencil
absolutely belongs to
TRACY DUBLINGER

! ! ! ! !

There is no way for
Principal Jones to know
this, but I do. Because I
pay attention to every detail.
Because *somebody* has to.

Of course, I want to tell Principal Jones about Tracy at this very minute, but she has just made it clear that she isn't going to be satisfied with only one piece of evidence.

For the eleventh time today, I catch myself wishing that Maude were here with me and, for the eleventh time, I remind myself that I am perfectly capable of doing this on my own.

"All right," says Principal Jones. "You can go back to class."

But now that Principal Jones and I are both on the same team, I decide to bring up something that has been bothering me.

Something has been bothering me.

Yes?

says Principal Jones.

I love being a detective. It's hard work, but I do it for the good of humanity.

Humanity?

It means "all the people."

I thought that Principal Jones was smarter than that.

She nods for me to continue, probably because she's embarrassed and just wants to move on.

And so I do. "But the truth is, I never work for free. I'd like to make an exception for you, of course, but I have to protect my reputation. I'm assuming you're familiar with my work in

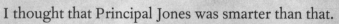

THE CASE of the MISSING LUNCH BOX?"

I am not.

That's kind of weird. It was a pretty big deal.

If I may ask, what is your rate?

Usually I charge — but given the severity of the crime and the importance of getting Eddie back, I decide to be aggressive.

Usually around two dollars, I say.

And sometimes three when the job is particularly **DANGEROUS.**

I pronounce every syllable of the word *dan-ger-ous* to make sure she understands I mean business.

Principal Jones wrinkles her forehead as if she had just taken a sip of old milk, and then she rubs her hands together as if she's trying to decide whether to feed me to her pet cougar.

Finally, she says,

Although I understand your dilemma—do you know what a dilemma is?

I nod. I am fairly certain that a dilemma is a kind of ferocious desert animal. I am surprised that Principal Jones thinks I might have one.

"Well then," she says, "although I do understand, I'm afraid that principals are not allowed to give money to students under *any circumstance*."

"Oh," I say.

I am disappointed, of course, but I suppose the rule makes sense. After all, if principals could pay kids for doing things, then Tammy and Tracy Dublinger would probably want to be paid for spelling words correctly, and Emily Estevez would have about a million dollars for being so nice and good and perfect all the time.

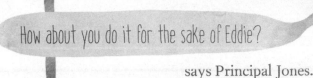

How about you do it for the sake of Eddie?

says Principal Jones.

In Volume 25:

Not Chinatown, Actual China,

Annabelle saves a baby panda that is trapped inside an abandoned jade mine and doesn't charge him a dime.

So I can live with the arrangement that Principal Jones is suggesting. Especially since what she is really saying is

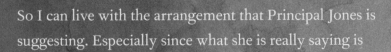

How about you do it for the sake of the Eddie Award?

Do we have a deal? she asks.

Deal.

I reach out to shake her
hand, and she shakes mine,
and her handshake is so FIRM

that I am a little bit
worried that all the bones in
my hand have been broken.

"You can go back to class now," she says.
But something else has been bothering
me, and so I keep sitting there.

"Before I go," I say, "I wonder if you
would be willing to call me Slim."

"Excuse me?" she says as if I have
just asked her to play checkers
with a meerkat.

KING ME, BABY!

138

It's my detective name, I say.

It would help if you would use it. Just until we crack this case.

I'm sorry, she says.

That's not possible.

I completely understand,

I say, though I think she's being pretty unreasonable.

Principal Jones starts to move around whatever important papers principals have to move around when they are not hanging students upside down by their ankles.

LIST OF STUDENTS TO HANG UPSIDE DOWN

EDDIE AN

CANDIC

NEW RU

TIPS FOR BETTER SCOWLIN

1. Squint

2. Keep yo Close

3. Alwa

4. Don

There's just one more thing.

What is it, Moxie?

I can tell from her voice that if I have any more questions for Principal Jones, I should probably wait at least a month before asking them. But this question is so important that I cannot help myself.

"As I leave your office, could you yell at me a little?"

"*Excuse* me?"

"I need to protect my cover," I say. "It's important that the other kids not know the real reason I'm here. If you could yell a little, they would assume I did some incredibly-brave-and-daring-though-technically-against-the-rules thing, and not that we're working together to solve this horrible crime."

"I see," she says. "Yes, of course. I would be delighted to yell at you."

She walks across the room and opens her office door.

AND DON'T EVER LET ME CATCH YOU DOING THAT AGAIN!!! she

says, much

more loudly than I

imagined she would. I am impressed

by how well Principal Jones does her job.

Tiddlywhump Elementary is in very good hands.

Sitting on the little
bench just outside the door
is a kid named Stan. When he
hears Principal Jones yell, he bursts
into tears. I give him a little pat on
the shoulder to let him know he's
going to be okay, even though I'm
pretty sure he's not.

CHAPTER 8: CRIMINAL MASTERMINDS

Mrs. Breath gives me a horrible

as she writes me a hall pass.

Clearly, she loves it when kids get in trouble and thinks she has the greatest job in the world because she gets to see it happen all day, every day, every week, nine months of the year.

Something tells me that when she gets home at night, she sits on her couch and makes scrapbooks about all the kids she made cry that day.

When I get back to class, Mrs. Bunyan gives me the deepest sort of *SCOWL.*

−1 OWL POINT

She dislikes nothing more than when students miss spelling tests. I show her my hall pass and give her a smile to let her know I'm really sorry (even though I'm absolutely not).

She takes away an Owl Point anyway— because I didn't come straight back to the classroom after recess.

That's two in one day! she says. One more and you'll earn a trip to the principal's office!

I consider telling Mrs. Bunyan that I have just come *from* the principal's office, where Principal Jones and I have been working together on a **TOP SECRET PLAN TO SOLVE** *the* **CRIME OF THE CENTURY.**

But I don't. Because I have important work to do. And because I do not want to lose another Owl Point.

It's a well-known Tiddlywhump fact that if you lose three Owl Points in one day, you get sent straight to Principal Jones.

Which is why I make such a point of always stopping at two.

I open my binder to take out my math homework and discover a folded piece of paper that someone must have slipped inside. It reads

Important Information! CONFIDENTIAL !! Read Right Away !!

My heart begins to pound.

Obviously, this has to do with the case. Maybe it is an anonymous tip from someone who saw Tracy stealing Eddie.

Or perhaps, knowing that I have her cornered, Tracy has written a full confession and has left it here for me!

I hadn't expected the case to be wrapped up this easily, but clearly my reputation precedes me. Glancing around the room to make sure no one is looking, I carefully unfold the note.

Dear Slim of M&? inc.-
    I would like to hire you to solve an important case. Moxie seems to have lost her comb. I hope you can help her find it. IT'S AN EMERGENCY !!!
                            Tracy

Of course I am tempted to run my fingers through my hair, but I do not want to give Tracy the satisfaction of thinking she has even sort of hurt my feelings, and so I fold up the note and slide it into my pocket and try very hard to distract myself by thinking about Maude.

Eventually, however, I can't stand it anymore and sneak the tiniest glance over at Tracy, who is looking right at me . . . while combing her long blond hair.

As Mrs. Bunyan starts handing back the graded spelling tests, I decide that my new life goal is making sure Tracy gets sent to the kind of prison that does not allow dental floss.

When Mrs. Bunyan gets to my desk, she smiles in a worrisome way and says, "You will be getting your own *special* set of words when you make up the test during second recess." She says the word *special* the way a police dog might growl at a burglar who has stolen the bishop's silver candelabra and is cornered in a dead-end alley.

I look over at Tracy just as Mrs. Bunyan is handing back her test. I try to read her expression as she looks at her grade, but her face is so perfectly blank that it's impossible to tell whether she failed or got a perfect score. Ditto Tammy. I see them both trying to look at each other's grades while pretending *not* to look at each other's grades.

Tracy is using one hand to cover her grade and her other hand to hold her . . . . purple pencil.

I *know* with 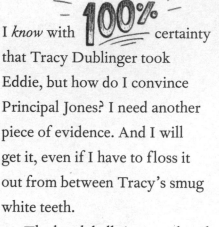 certainty that Tracy Dublinger took Eddie, but how do I convince Principal Jones? I need another piece of evidence. And I will get it, even if I have to floss it out from between Tracy's smug white teeth.

The lunch bell rings, and we head to the cafeteria. The Dublingers sit where they always do, directly across from each other and as close as possible to a table full of sixth-grade boys.

I will deal with Tracy in a minute, but first I need to check on Milton. It's the last thing I feel like doing, but I promised Mom. Plus, I figure it might cheer him up to know I've made progress on the case.

Milton is sitting next to his friend Avery. I give Avery a look. Not a mean look, exactly, but an *it's probably better that you sit somewhere else for about five minutes because I have to talk to my brother* kind of look.

149

The look works. Avery moves down a few seats. He doesn't actually cry, but I can tell he's considering it.

I sit down next to Milton, who is chewing with determination.

It wasn't Bob, I tell him.

He CHEWS and CHEWS and CHEWS and eventually swallows.

"I know," he says.

"You *know*?"

"Bob is left-handed."

"So?"

"The greasy fingerprint was on the *left* side of the knob," says Milton. "Bob ate the doughnuts with his *left* hand. If he had opened the case, the thumbprint would have been on the *right* side."

"I know that," I say. And I do know it, of course. I have just been too busy dealing with the pressures of managing such an important case to connect that particular detail. It's the sort of thing that Maude would have figured out instantly.

How did you know about Bob's doughnuts? I ask.

Bob eats doughnuts at recess every day, says Milton.

Usually glazed, but sometimes chocolate, and every once in a while strawberry cream. He always keeps them in his left coat pocket.

Part of me is impressed, and the other part thinks Milton should spend more time playing at recess and less time studying Bob Tuttleman's secret snacking habits.

I decide that it's probably best not to tell Milton about my conversation with Principal Jones.

Except that I am very proud of it.

"I am working with Principal Jones to solve the crime," I say.

"Really?" asks Milton, wiping the lens of his glasses with his shirt. Clearly, he is very impressed.

"Yes," I say. "And while I was in her office, I discovered another clue."

What is it?

says Milton.

I know he is excited, but even when he's excited, Milton is about as lively as a tired turtle. When he's not excited, he is about as lively as a dead turtle.

I tell Milton about the purple pencil, and even before I can tell him I think Tracy Dublinger did it, he says,

So you think Tracy Dublinger did it.

I suppose I shouldn't be surprised. Tracy Dublinger's opinion of purple pencils is so well known that even first graders are aware of it.

"Isn't it obvious?" I say.

"Maybe," says Milton. "But there are other people who use purple pencils."

"Who?" I ask.

"I'm just saying it's possible."

I want to point out that it's also possible an ostrich will suddenly crash through the lunchroom window playing a flügelhorn, but I decide to keep this observation to myself, because Milton looks like he's on the verge of figuring something out.

What else can you tell me about the pencil? asks Milton.

It had a bunch of little bite marks all along the sides.

Hmm . . .

I wish that Milton would say something more helpful than *Hmm*.

Did you tell Principal Jones that Tracy did it?

*Nope. We need to find another piece of evidence.
It's very important not to jump to conclusions.*

Milton looks at me as if I've just said something really wise.

That's true.

I just need to figure out where Tracy stashed Eddie.

If she took Eddie.

I give Milton a pat on the back. I admire him for trying so hard. He is a smart kid, but there's so much he doesn't know about the world. He's just in first grade. He cannot ride a unicycle. And he doesn't have an insect named after him.

This problem isn't going to be solved by standing here chatting with Milton. I need to talk to the owl thief herself.

"I need you to do me a favor," I say. "My hair. Does it look okay?"

Milton looks at me as if I've asked him to climb Mount Kilimanjaro.

"It hasn't fallen out or anything."

"Is it straight?"

"I think so."

"Is it or isn't it?"

"A few of your hairs might be a little bit sideways."

"Could you smooth them out?"

"Do I have to?"

"*Yes.*"

"Will it help you find Eddie?"

"It absolutely will."

155

Milton reaches over and kind of pushes my hair around. It is impossible that he has made the situation on top of my head any better, but I think of what Mom might say, and it goes something like this:

Whether your hair is straight or 100% messed up, you are still 100% you, which is 100% great. Maybe even 110%.

WHICH IS TO SAY,

LOOK OUT, TRACY DUBLINGER!

I give Avery a little nod to let him know that he can move back to his original seat, but from the look on his face, I get the sense he feels more comfortable staying down there at the far end of the bench.

I take a deep breath and walk over to where Tracy and Tammy are sitting. They seem to be sharing

ONE GIGANTIC SANDWICH,

each eating from an opposite end and handing it back and forth between bites. I do not plan on sticking around long enough to see what happens when they get to the middle.

I decide to "go for the jugular," which is how Annabelle Adams describes what she does when she knows who committed the crime and is trying to find that critical piece of information she needs to prove it. I do not entirely know what a jugular is, but that is not going to stop me from going for it.

Hey, Tracy,

I say with the extremely calm and self-confident demeanor of someone who does not care in the slightest what her hair looks like.

Can I borrow your *purple pencil?*

Tracy looks at me as if I've just asked to borrow her underwear.

No way,

she says.

She won't even let *me* use her purple pencil,

says Tammy.

And I'm her favorite person in the world.

*Second-*favorite,

says Tracy, correcting her sister.

I wonder for a moment who Tracy Dublinger's #1 favorite person is. But then I realize, of course, it's

I
decide
to keep
pressing my
point. "I just
wanted to
make sure
you still have
your *purple pencil*," I say.
"I want to make sure
that you didn't, for
example, *drop it* somewhere when
you were *doing something or other* on your
way to the nurse's office this morning."

I suppose you could argue that I'm being pretty obvious, but
I want to make sure Tracy knows that I'm onto her, that there's
no escape, and that the best thing to do is to make a full confession
and turn herself in to the authorities this very minute.

But she doesn't squirm. She doesn't look the slightest bit
guilty. In addition to being a criminal mastermind, Tracy
Dublinger is one of the finest liars I have ever encountered.

Could you please move along, *Moxie?* says Tracy, flicking her wrist as if she were waving away a swarm of gnats.

You're blocking the view.

Tracy is looking over my shoulder at something, and so I turn to look, and that something is Darrin Duncan, an oversized sixth grader with long arms and bushy eyebrows who has been described to me as

I can't even pretend to know what that means.

I decide to leave the Dublingers to their sandwich and their view. As far as I am concerned, I have more than enough evidence to put Tracy behind bars until she is 93 years old.

I head back to let Milton know that I'm on my way to see Principal Jones. When I walk up to the table, Avery spills his milk. And then he starts crying.

It isn't Tracy's pencil,

says Milton before I can open my mouth.

Of course it is,

I say.

It's *obvious*.

There's no way that someone who cares so much about her teeth would have chewed on her pencil like that.

I feel like I've been punched in the gut. But as much as I hate to admit it, Milton is probably right. Tracy is neat and proper in every way and always keeps her desk and school supplies incredibly tidy and organized. I once saw her get offended when someone sneezed on the other side of the room.

The mere thought of getting flecks of purple paint stuck between her perfect molars would be enough to send Tracy off the deep end.

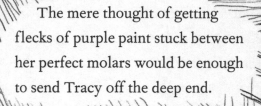

But **IF** the purple pencil isn't Tracy's,

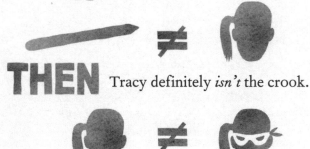

THEN Tracy definitely *isn't* the crook.

I am devastated. Tracy seems *so much* like an owl thief. But a true detective knows not to argue with the evidence. So I take out my notebook and cross off her name, confident that she will commit some *other* awful crime soon enough.

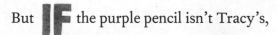

PRIME
SUSPECTS

✓ 1. ~~BOB~~
✓ 2. LEON
✓ 3. ~~TRACY~~
4. EMILY

If Tracy didn't do it and Bob didn't do it, there are only two remaining possibilities: the perfect and wholesome Emily Estevez and the bizarre and brainwashed Leon Magruder.

I glance over at Emily. She is slumped over the lunchroom table, her head resting on her arms, which are folded in front of her.

Her tray is right next to her, food untouched.

I'd go over and continue my interrogation, but I'm not sure I have the heart to wake her up again.

On the one hand, if I could prove that Emily stole Eddie, the Eddie Award would be mine.

On the other hand, it seems impossible that Emily would do something like this. She's just so GOOD.

And she really dislikes soup.

She'd make such an excellent friend.

But I'm starting to wonder if, rather than try to find a replacement for Maude, I should just go it on my own for a while. I've learned from Annabelle Adams that friends can get in the way of the cold-blooded decisions one has to make to be a top-notch detective.

In Volume 2:

ROSE-COLORED GLASSES,

Annabelle has to choose between saving her best friend, ELEANOR, from a burning lighthouse and rescuing a group of KINDERGARTNERS from a sinking tugboat.

She saves everyone, of course, because she is Annabelle Adams, but she saves the kindergartners *first*, which makes Eleanor so angry that she eventually joins forces with Annabelle's sworn nemesis, Dr. Fungo—but not before gaining incredible strength after being bitten by a radioactive otter.

HMS FUNGO

165

Which is a long way of saying that—for the time being, at least—it's probably best that I *don't* get too close to Emily. The stakes are too high.

But if you tied me to a tree

and threatened to let fire ants

lick peanut butter

off my kneecaps

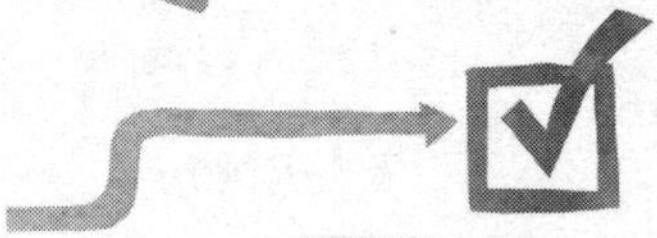

until I agreed to pick out a new best friend,

Emily is the person

I would be most likely to invite over

to play croquet

and *not* eat a steaming bowl of clam chowder.

I am an excellent judge of character, and my gut says that

EMILY IS INNOCENT.

Which means there is really just one remaining suspect.

Leon is sitting by himself at the far end of the lunchroom. He has spread his mashed potatoes out across his tray and is drawing in them with his finger.

I sit down across the table from Leon and give him my most intimidating stare. But he doesn't look up.

"Hey, Leon," I say.

There's so much POW, ZAP, and ZOWEE going on that I don't even know if he can hear me.

"Hey, Leon," I say again.

A little glob of mashed potato flies off Leon's finger and hits me on the elbow.

"Hey, LEON." This time Leon *does* look up, as if he's being interrupted by a very important person from another country.

"Uh, what?" he says.

"I need to ask you a few questions," I say.

"Okay," he says.

He seems excited.

"What are you doing with your potatoes?" I ask.

"Oh man," he says. "Oh man, oh man. I am working on a new comic about a superhero.

He is part chicken and part hamster and part motorcycle and part lemonade and part—"

"Leon . . ."

"Yeah?"

"What do you know about the disappearance of our beloved mascot, Eddie?"

"What?" he says, blinking at me in the way that criminals do when they are trying to pretend that they have no idea what you're talking about.

"Do you mean to say that you don't know that Eddie has been stolen?" I ask.

Is Eddie that owl?

168

I can feel my blood beginning to **BOIL.** For a fourth-grade student at Tiddlywhump Elementary, not knowing who Eddie is might be a worse crime than stealing him.

I try to stay calm.

You seem a little nervous, Leon, I say.

Why is that?

One of my pencils is missing. It's very upsetting.

I look at the tray of pencils sitting next to Leon. It is a set of two dozen or so colored pencils, and one of them is, in fact, missing.

Oh, that's *terrible,* I say.

Sometimes, with criminals, you have to make them think you're on their side so that they will get comfortable and slip up and accidentally give you important information.

One time, in

Annabelle spends an entire week
living in an igloo and sharing whale
blubber with a bank robber just
to find out his mother's maiden name.

"*Which* pencil is missing?" I say as innocently as a five-year-old on the first day of kindergarten.

"The most important one," says Leon. "The *purple* one!"

I glance down at the set of pencils. All of them are different colors. It's like looking through a prism. But the purple one is not where it should be. And then I notice something else—*all* the pencils have been chewed up.

"Let me see your teeth, Magruder," I say.

Leon flashes me a huge, toothy grin, and when he does, I see all the colors of the rainbow. Tiny flecks of pencil paint dot every tooth in his mouth.

170

Leon has just moved from mere suspect to **PUBLIC ENEMY #1.**

Clearly, I am looking at the owl thief! Now I have to change my tactics. Now I need to get him to admit to actually stealing Eddie!

"Could you say that again?" I say. "Which of your pencils is missing?"

The PURPLE one, says Leon.

THE PURPLE ONE!

Oh, how I wish that I had a tiny recording device hidden inside my earring like Annabelle Adams does!

"What if I were to tell you that your pencil has been found?" I say.

"You found my pencil?" says Leon. He is very excited.

Now is the time for my nice-guy routine to end.

I have Leon right where I want him.

"It was found at the *scene of the crime*!" I say.

"There was a CRIME?" Leon's eyes light up. Clearly, I'm speaking his language. "Who DID IT?"

Don't play dumb, Magruder. But Leon doesn't even hear me.

171

Was it Doctor Oblivion?

The Killer Koala?

The Popsicle Pirate?

Leon is in orbit again, and I'm not sure how to get him back to Earth so that I can continue my interrogation.

When Maude and I were teaming up to solve a case, I would start things off by being mean and loud and terrifying to rattle the suspect, and then she would come in and be nice and calm and friendly, so that whoever we were interrogating would feel relieved and get comfortable and suddenly give away some critical piece of information that would basically solve the case. But Maude is not here, and I don't know what to do.

How did you lose your pencil, Leon?

asks a voice from behind me.

It's Milton. I have no idea how long he's been standing there. "I've got this under control, Milton," I say. Once again, he is ruining my investigation.

Did you have it on your way to the principal's office?

He says it calmly, which would be the right approach if he had been invited to participate in this interrogation. But all of a sudden, Leon does seem more calm. For example, he is actually looking at Milton. I decide to see how this plays out. Even though he doesn't know it, Milton is doing a pretty good job of filling Maude's nice-guy shoes.

Did you have your pencil on your way to the principal's office?

says Milton again, even more patiently this time. Leon looks at me and then at Milton and then at me and then at Milton. He is blinking a little.

Did you have it on your way to the principal's office?

Milton asks for the third time.
This time something in Leon clicks.

Yes,

he says.

Did you have it on your way back from the principal's office?

Leon blinks a few more times.

No.

He pauses for a second, and his eyes light up as if he has just invented the fork.

No! When I got to Principal Jones's office . . . my pencil was *missing!*

I decide that it's time for a little more mean and loud.

Where did you go

once you left Mrs. Bunyan's classroom?

I am leaning over Leon and sticking my nose in his face. It is not pleasant, but it's necessary.

"To Principal Jones's office," he says. I can tell he's getting worried.

"Did you stop anywhere along the way?"

"I . . . I . . ."

"Did you, by any chance, pay a visit to Eddie, our beloved school mascot?" I ask, not very quietly at this point.

"I did," says Leon. "I guess I'd never noticed him before. But he was so cute I couldn't help myself."

NEWS

Leon has just admitted to being at the crime scene!

FLASH

Was it before or after morning announcements?

asks Milton.

It's time for a little more nice guy now. I have to say, Milton's instincts are pretty good.

175

"It was exactly *during* morning announcements," says Leon. "I was standing by the case, and morning announcements came on, and that loud buzz startled me so much that I . . . I . . ."

"Dropped your pencil?" says Milton with the calm and kindness of a friendly grandfather.

"Yes!" says Leon. "That's *exactly* what happened."

Right before you stole Eddie?

I ask, leaning in like a hurricane that is about to send 40-foot waves crashing down on Leon's head.

I'd never steal anything!

says Leon.

I fight for the forces of good!

Milton is pulling on his right earlobe with that faraway look in his eye.

As I stand there wondering whether I should go get Principal Jones,

call 9-1-1,

or put Leon in a choke hold, Leon reaches into his pocket and pulls out a little tub of lip balm. But instead of rubbing it on his lips with his finger like any normal person on the planet would, he does it

with his *thumb*. His *right* thumb. His *greasy* right thumb.

I realize I have all the evidence I need to prove Leon stole Eddie.

177

Thanks, Milton,

I say as I rush out of the cafeteria.

Wait!

he says.

But there is no time for chitchat. I only have a few minutes to find Principal Jones before lunch period ends.

I'll see you at second recess,

I say.

If I'm even at *second recess*, I think. Once I let Principal Jones know that Leon took Eddie, it's possible that she will give me the rest of the day off. It's possible that she will give *everyone* the rest of the day off.

Wait, Moxie!

It is really touching how much Milton loves me, but I simply do not have time to talk to him right now. I have a criminal to expose, an owl to rescue, and a school to save.

CHAPTER 9: THE ENEMY OF PROGRESS

When I get to Principal
Jones's office, Mrs.
Breath is bent over
her computer and
typing so fast and
loud that I wonder
if she's trying to win
some kind of prize—
or maybe to drill through the center of the planet.

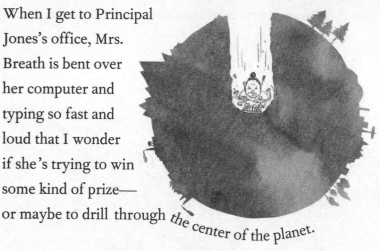

I stand there for a moment, trying to get her attention.
Then I make a few loud coughs, and when that doesn't
work, I fake a sneeze. But she still does not look up.

So I just say it. "I need to see Principal Jones."

Mrs. Breath looks up. "Excuse me?" she says. She looks
at me as if she just spotted a herd of wildebeest in the
girls' bathroom.

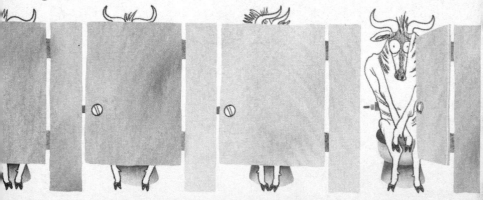

"Principal Jones," I say again. "I have something important to tell her."

Mrs. Breath gives me a horrible smile. "I'm sorry," she says, although she definitely isn't. "Principal Jones is busy right now."

I assume that someone or other is treading water in the eel tank at this exact moment and that Principal Jones needs to finish up before she can talk to me.

"I'll wait," I say, sitting down on the extremely uncomfortable bench.

"You will not wait!" Mrs. Breath stands up to show me how tall she is, which doesn't work very well, since she is basically the shortest adult I have ever seen in my life.

GO BACK TO CLASS THIS INSTANT!

It is clear that spending any more time in the same room as Mrs. Breath is not going to be good for my health, so I leave.

I think about how strange it is that when kids *don't* want to see the principal, they get sent to the principal, but when they really *need* to see the principal, it's impossible to actually do it. And then I have an idea. The *perfect* idea. I run back to class as fast as I can.

I have learned from Annabelle Adams that sometimes you have to do the exact *opposite* of what common sense suggests.

In Volume 15:

The Harder They Fall, Annabelle plays dead to survive an encounter with an angry hot dog vendor,

and in Volume 30:

The Better to See You With, Annabelle disguises herself as a blind fortune-teller so she can sneak into the secret chamber where the Riddle of the Seven Horsemen is written on the walls.

I know what I want, but I cannot get it directly. Fortunately, there is another way.

I return to Mrs. Bunyan's classroom just as everyone else is settling in for an exciting lecture on single-stream recycling.

But instead of sitting down at my desk, I run right up to Mrs. Bunyan and give her a hug. A big, enthusiastic, long *Gosh, I really love you* kind of super hug. It is just about the last thing in the world that I want to do, but I need to lose an Owl Point as quickly as I can, and my hug has *exactly* the effect I am hoping for.

First Mrs. Bunyan turns white. Then bright pink. Then the deepest red. She is so surprised that she can't even speak.

The class is amazed and also terrified.

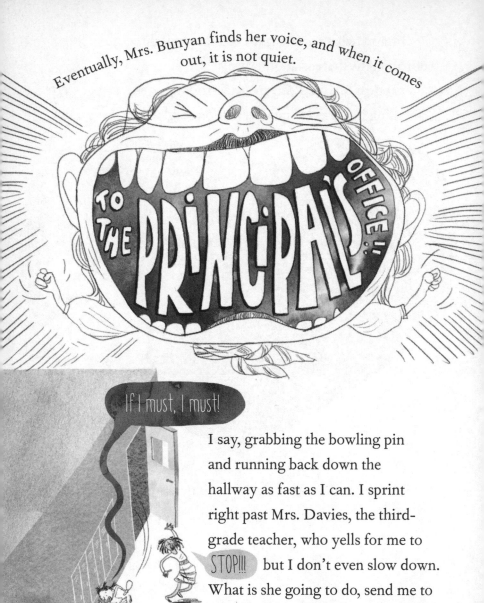

Eventually, Mrs. Bunyan finds her voice, and when it comes out, it is not quiet.

"TO THE PRINCIPAL'S OFFICE!!"

If I must, I must!

I say, grabbing the bowling pin and running back down the hallway as fast as I can. I sprint right past Mrs. Davies, the third-grade teacher, who yells for me to STOP!!! but I don't even slow down. What is she going to do, send me to the principal's office?

I burst back into the main office, and there is Mrs. Breath. She opens her mouth, but before she can say whatever awful thing has just popped into her head, I show her the bowling pin, and all the wind goes out of her.

She looks at me as if she were a hungry tiger and I were a juicy steak on the other side of a

THICK GLASS WALL.

She pushes a button on her phone.

Moxie McCoy has been sent to see you.

I hear the exasperated voice of Principal Jones.

Send her in.

A moment later, I am sitting on Principal Jones's bench. She does not look happy to see me.

"What did you do?" she asks.

"Oh, I didn't actually get in trouble," I say.

"It looks like you did," she says, gesturing to the bowling pin.

"Yes, but I got in trouble on *purpose*," I say. "I needed to see you right away."

Principal Jones raises one of her eyebrows. Just one. I am extremely jealous. I have been practicing for years and cannot do it.

"And why is that?" says Principal Jones.

"To discuss the case," I say. "I know who took Eddie."

Principal Jones sits back in her chair and lets out a sigh. She looks skeptical at best, but I can tell that there is just a glimmer of hope in her eye. She knows that Tiddlywhump Elementary is basically nothing without our beloved mascot.

"And you have solid evidence this time?" she asks.

"Absolutely," I say.

"Before you speak," she says, "it is very important that you do not accuse someone of stealing Eddie unless you are

ENTIRELY CERTAIN.

I hope you've learned your lesson."

"Oh, I have," I say.

"I want you to be so certain that there is no room for doubt."

I think of what Annabelle Adams always says in situations like this:

Perfection is the enemy of progress.

And what she means is that the world is so strange and confusing and unpredictable that you can never be 100% certain about anything, but that you must always do your very best to get as close to the truth as you can. Which is what I always try to do at every moment.

But I'm pretty sure Principal Jones hasn't read the entire Annabelle Adams series 37½ times.

"No doubt at all," I say.

All right, she says, sitting straight up in her chair, folding her arms, and breathing just a little bit of fire to let me know there's way more where that came from.

Who do you think stole Eddie?

This time, instead of starting by giving Principal Jones the name of the crook, I build my case by laying out the evidence.

First of all, the criminal—

The suspect, she reminds me.

Of course she is right. Leon is not technically a criminal until he is proven to be a criminal. Which is just about to happen.

"First of all, the *suspect* has greasy fingers because he puts on lip balm using his thumb! Which is why he left the greasy thumbprint on Eddie's case."

"I see," says Principal Jones, who is obviously not yet convinced. "Go on."

It belongs to the owl thief, who dropped it near Eddie's case while committing the crime.

I pause for a moment to build suspense.

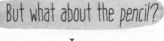

It belongs to . . . LEON MAGRUDER!

I say this the way a magician might say "Aha!" when he pulls back his handkerchief and the rabbit has suddenly appeared in his hat.

But Principal Jones does not seem amazed. "I'm afraid you don't have any actual evidence," she says.

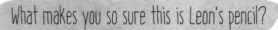

But what about the *pencil?*

I say.

What makes you so sure this is Leon's pencil?

Because of the bite marks!

I say.

Leon does that to all his pencils!

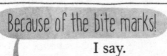

I am suddenly sorry that I did not grab the rest of Leon's pencils when I had the chance. I could have compared the bite marks and collected the DNA!

But more important, the suspect dropped his pencil—*that* pencil—right by Eddie's case in the middle of committing the crime!

I say, pointing to the pencil on Principal Jones's desk.

This pencil?

says Principal Jones, picking up the chewed-up purple pencil from her desk.

That pencil,

I say.

What do you know about this pencil?

she asks.

I explain that I overheard her conversation with Mr. Hammer, and that my keen detective sense tells me the pencil almost certainly belongs to the person who nabbed Eddie.

"Eavesdropping is a serious offense," she tells me.

"I definitely wasn't eavesdropping," I say. "I was just *collecting evidence*." Principal Jones sort of—halfway but not quite—smiles again.

"And what does the pencil have to do with Eddie?"

 **Like this?** she says.

Principal Jones picks up a yellow pencil and puts it sideways in her mouth. Then she bites it over and over and over again. Within a few seconds, it looks just as chewed up as Leon's pencil.

"I see your point," I say. "But Mr. Hammer found a *purple* pencil, which is exactly the color of pencil that was missing from Leon's set!"

Principal Jones opens her desk drawer and pulls out a small, flat box. Inside the box are . . . eight brand-new purple pencils.

"Hmmm," I say.

"Can you be *absolutely sure* that Leon did this?" she asks.

My first thought is that perhaps PRINCIPAL JONES is the one who stole Eddie, but my second thought is that this is a ridiculous thought. My third thought is that I know *in my gut* that the pencil belongs to Leon. It is *without a doubt* the pencil that was missing from his set.

I guess I can't prove *for sure* that Leon is the one who dropped the pencil near Eddie's case. But who else would have? Who else *could* have?

"I can be *almost* absolutely sure," I say.

"Well," says Principal Jones, "I am absolutely sure that Leon did *not* take Eddie."

"Why?" I ask, because it seems literally impossible that Leon is not the culprit.

"As a punishment for being disruptive during class, I asked Leon to help Mr. Hammer set up chairs for the assembly, which he was still doing when I discovered that Eddie was missing."

"Oh," I say, suddenly as confused as I have ever been.

I want to ask whether the setting-up-chairs part happened before or after the more awful and interesting forms of punishment, but it seems like the wrong time.

Just then, Principal Jones's phone makes the beeping sound again. I brace myself as the voice of Mrs. Breath fills the room.

He's here.

Principal Jones presses a button on her phone.

Thank you. We'll be done in just a minute,

she says without taking her eyes off me.

Principal Jones looks at me with a stare so deep and long it feels like she's trying to memorize my insides.

Tell me about your brother,

she says.

My brother?

Yes, Milton. What can you tell me about him?

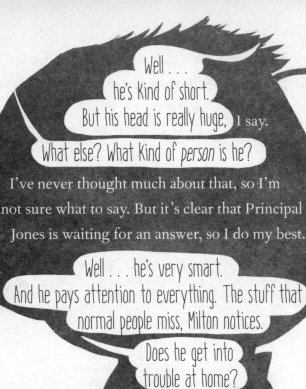

Well . . .
he's kind of short.
But his head is really huge, I say.

What else? What kind of *person* is he?

I've never thought much about that, so I'm
not sure what to say. But it's clear that Principal
Jones is waiting for an answer, so I do my best.

Well . . . he's very smart.
And he pays attention to everything. The stuff that
normal people miss, Milton notices.

Does he get into
trouble at home?

Never.
He'd never break a rule.

Does he tell the truth?

Always.

It sounds like you're pretty lucky to have a brother like that,

she says with a kind, wise look that makes me
suspect she's probably not just a principal but
also somebody's mom.

I sit there for a second and let her words sink in. It had never occurred to me until this moment, but she's right. I am lucky to have a brother like Milton.

An instant later, Principal Jones switches back to full-on principal mode.

Let me make myself clear. You are not to spend another moment on this *case,*

she tells me, saying "case" as if my case were a bag full of fish heads she is setting by the curb.

I will figure out who took Eddie, and *you* will focus on being a fourth grader.

I know that Principal Jones is just saying this because it is the sort of thing that a principal *has* to say and that she is only speaking this loudly because she wants to impress Mrs. Breath and whatever kids are sitting on the bench outside her office.

I am a trained detective. She is just a principal who lacks the skills and experience required for a case of this magnitude. But she has to protect her reputation.

"Do you understand me?"

"Of course," I say. "Thank you for your assistance."

"Excuse me?" she says. She is doing a really good job of pretending to be angry with me. It's what makes her such an outstanding principal.

I think I'll go back to class now,

I say.

I think that's an *excellent* idea,

she says.

And do not forget what I said.

She looks at me as if she's a bow and arrow and I'm the circle in the center of the target.

"Principal Jones," I say, "could you please remember to yell at me a little as I leave your office?"

AND WHAT IS IT THAT YOU THINK I'VE BEEN **DOING** FOR THE LAST FIVE MINUTES?

"That was perfect," I say as I slip out the door.

There, on the little bench directly across from Mrs. Breath's desk is a kid who sort of halfway looks like Milton. I almost walk right by, but then I look again and can't believe my eyes. It *is* Milton.

What are *you* doing here?

I ask.

Seeing him there is like seeing a snowman on the sun.

Mr. Brightenhouse said Principal Jones wanted to talk to me, so here I am.

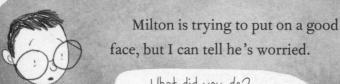

Milton is trying to put on a good face, but I can tell he's worried.

What did you *do*?

I ask. I'm trying to make sense of it.

I have no idea.

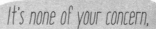

It's none of your concern,

says Mrs. Breath, practically gloating as she hands me a hall pass and points to the door.

Get back to class this instant!

I reach over and squeeze Milton's hand.

It's going to be okay, whatever it is.

He nods back at me. He's never looked so sad and small.

BACK TO CLASS!

roars Mrs. Breath.

I go. I fear for our safety if I don't. I glance over my shoulder just as Milton disappears into Principal Jones's office.

As I walk back to Mrs. Bunyan's classroom, my mind is spinning. My beloved mascot is missing. My best friend is not here when I need her most. And now my defenseless little brother is walking into the lion's den.

I do my best not to panic, but I can't shake the feeling that this bad day just got so much worse.

CHAPTER 10: THE INTERROGATION

When I get back to class, Mrs. Bunyan is not even sort of happy to see me, but I slip into my chair and try to look as innocent as I possibly can. For the time being, I am back to *not* wanting to be sent to the principal's office.

I review my list of suspects. There are four names. All but one is crossed out. If it isn't Bob or Tracy or Leon, it must be . . .

PRIME SUSPECTS

1. BOB
2. LEON
3. TRACY
4. EMILY !!!

As Mrs. Bunyan switches from recycling to making thrilling observations about igneous rocks, I glance over at Emily. She is slumped over her desk, holding up her head with both of her hands as if it weighed a thousand pounds. She looks anxious and pale. Usually Emily Estevez looks as adorable and happy as a basket of baby seals. But at this moment, she looks . . . could it be . . .  GUILTY?

Maybe, just maybe, instead of being the greatest and the nicest and the best, Emily Estevez is nothing but a two-faced liar and owl thief. It's hard to accept that I could have been so wrong about her, but the evidence suggests that Emily has been fooling me—and everyone else—this entire time.

I look at the clock. It's almost time for second recess.

I need to find Milton and figure out what Principal Jones wanted from him.

And I need to interrogate Emily and see if I can figure out where she has hidden Eddie.

But second recess is only 20 minutes long, so I'll have to work fast.

The bell rings and I grab my jacket. I'm about to race out to the playground, when I run into Mrs. Bunyan, who is standing by the classroom door with her arms folded. She looks at me with a dour smirk and speaks the two words I least want to hear.

SPELLING TEST.

She points to my desk. My heart sinks as I come to terms with the fact that there is no escape.

I sit and take out a piece of paper. I brace myself for the worst.

When Mrs. Bunyan gives spelling tests, she reads words aloud from a piece of paper, and we write them down. But Mrs. Bunyan isn't holding a piece of paper.

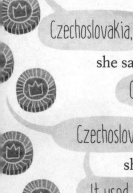

Czechoslovakia,

she says.

Checkers of what?

Czechoslovakia,

she says again.

It used to be a country in Europe.

Is that a fourth-grade vocabulary word?

I ask as politely as I can.

It is today,

she says.

If it is possible for someone to smile while frowning, that is what Mrs. Bunyan is doing at this moment. This is like Christmas for her. Christmas mixed with Halloween mixed with Easter morning. I am the big chocolate bunny in her basket, and Mrs. Bunyan is going to eat me in one bite.

With a clear head on a normal day, I would file an official protest with the mayor, but today I am preoccupied with the fate of one 35-pound human being, who at this precise moment could be getting his eyeballs licked by eels.

I do my best to write down whatever it is that Mrs. Bunyan said.

1. checkers of lockeeya

"Next word, please."

But Mrs. Bunyan is in no rush. Now she is holding her dictionary and leafing slowly through the pages, making little happy sounds like "Hmm" and "Ooh" and "Ha-ha-ha," as if she were filling her plate at an endless buffet.

It seems like hours pass before her eyes light up and she says, with absolute glee,

Bougainvillea.

I'm pretty sure this is that kind of purple rash that Arnie Butler once got on his backside, and I do my best to spell it.

"Next, please," I say.

"Ricochet."

Finally, I catch a break. I actually know Rick. Nice fellow. *And* I know how to spell his name. It seems like a really weird word for a spelling test, but at least I'll get *one* question right.

Next, please.

1. checkers of lockeeya

2. booganveela

3. Rick O'Shea

This goes on and on for so long that it feels like

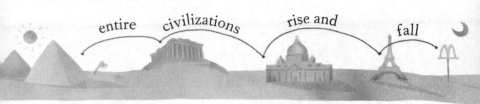

entire civilizations rise and fall

as Mrs. Bunyan punishes me with impossible words and impossible slowness. I take it with grim poise, just like Annabelle Adams in Volume 53: *Not Very Bon Appetit,* in which Dr. Fungo captures Annabelle, puts her in a dismal tower, and forces her to eat nothing but bugs, slugs, and spiders for an entire year.

But instead of getting grossed out and wasting away to nothing, Annabelle learns how to cook these things into delicious casseroles, smoothies, and pies and publishes a bestselling cookbook three weeks after she escapes.

Which is to say, if *she* can make it through her ordeal, so can I.

"Another word, please," I say as cheerfully as I can.

"ONOMATOPOEIA," says Mrs. Bunyan.

It hits me like a tidal wave. But it does not knock me over.

Moxie
McCoy

1. checkers of lockeeya
2. booganveela
3. Rick O'Shea
4. ideerowsinkorsee
5. ottermotterpeer
6. trisketdeska photograph
7. tear a dactell
8. suedunim
9. rondayvoo
10. new monick

What feels like fourteen hours later, I write the last word and hand in my test. Mrs. Bunyan actually licks her lips as she takes my paper.

"Can I go now?" I ask as politely as I can.

"You *may*," she says. I look at the clock. I have five minutes left.

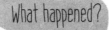

I sprint outside. I *want* to interrogate Emily, but I *need* to talk to Milton.

For once, I am relieved to see him in his thinking spot. It's far better than finding him in Mrs. Breath's private dungeon.

What happened?

What did she say?

Are you all right?

Did you get hung upside down by your ankles?

Somebody told Principal Jones I kidnapped Eddie.

WHAT?

WHO?

WHY?

"Apparently, it was an anonymous tip—written in a note."

"A note?"

"A note. Saying I had stolen Eddie and was wearing his bow tie."

"But you wore that bow tie this morning! You wear a bow tie EVERY DAY!"

"That's what I told Principal Jones."

"Did she believe you?"

"I'm not sure. I think so."

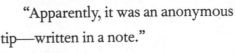

What happens now?

Whoever it was said they had

ADDITIONAL EVIDENCE.

Additional evidence?

Additional evidence that would be "revealed at the proper moment."

I don't usually think of myself as an aggressive person, but I'm ready to drop-kick whoever did this over Ample Creek.

Principal Jones said I could go back to class, and that she'd let me know if she needed me again.

A horrible thought occurs to me.

DID YOU LOSE AN OWL POINT?

Not yet.

WHEW! Okay ... well ... what do we do now?

Wait, I guess.

I grab Milton by both of his shoulders and look him directly in the eye.

WE WILL NOT WAIT. We will figure out who DID steal Eddie so that we can prove that person was NOT you!

That does sound better than waiting,

says Milton, and it's almost impossible to tell, but I think he's smiling just a little.

I take a few deep breaths. At the moment, I am the opposite of calm.

"I do know one thing for sure. It *wasn't* Leon," I say.

"I know," says Milton.

"How do *you* know?

Leon dropped his pencil at Eddie's case *during* morning announcements, says Milton.

I went to the bathroom right *after* morning announcements,

and Eddie was still in his case.

So Leon couldn't have taken him.

Eddie's case is right around the corner from the first-grade classroom. Milton has told me that every time he goes, he always sneaks a quick peek, just to pay his respects.

"Why didn't you tell me?" I ask. Milton can be so *frustrating*!

"I tried to," he says. "Twice."

I vaguely remember Milton saying something or other as I ran out of the cafeteria.

I consider being angry with him for not trying harder, but there simply isn't time.

"That leaves Emily as the last remaining suspect," I say.

"I don't think it was her," says Milton. "Emily has always been so nice to me."

I tell Milton that Emily has always been nice to *everyone*—that it's her smoke screen. That she has only been *pretending* to be good and kind and lovable so that she can fool us all at this very moment.

It suddenly occurs to me that Emily has been nice and good as long as I have known her. Is it possible that she has been planning this crime since *kindergarten*? I suddenly have a whole new appreciation for my adversary.

We have to figure out how to prove Emily took Eddie.

I say this in part because I like how it sounds, but in part because when Maude and I were trying to puzzle through a mystery,

I'd state the facts,

and it would help her connect the dots. Milton did such a good job filling in for Maude when I interrogated Leon that I'm hoping he'll be able to do the same now.

But instead of making useful observations, he just stands there, pulling on his right earlobe and looking miserable.

It isn't Emily,

he says.

It just can't be.

I want to tell Milton that there's no room for emotions when it comes to solving crimes.

In Volume 48:

The Really Bad Breakfast,

Annabelle Adams discovers that it was *her own grandmother* who had stolen the

QUEEN'S JEWELS.

But she still took her to Scotland Yard, which is where all the worst criminals in England are taken when they get caught.

If you ask me, British criminals are pretty lucky to get to hang out in a yard. But I don't have time to go into that right now.

"It can't be her," says Milton again.

I show him the page from my notebook with the list of suspects and only Emily's name remaining.

"I'm afraid it is," I say. I don't want to rush him, but second recess will be ending soon, and I need *something*—a new clue or a new angle—I can use to get Emily to crack.

Suddenly, I have an idea. Even if Emily is a criminal mastermind, there's no reason why we can't use her problem-solving technique—which is exactly what happens in Volume 14: *Poetic Justice*, when Annabelle steals the Atomic Lake Evaporator Dr. Fungo invented to ruin summer vacations around the world and uses it instead to evaporate all the water in his swimming pool just as he is leaping from the really high diving board. Dr. Fungo lands on a pool float, bounces over the fence, and escapes, but the point remains that it's perfectly fine to use someone's diabolical invention or problem-solving technique against them *as long as it will help your case.*

"Why is January?" I say.

Milton's eyes get wide. I can tell he approves, so I say it again.

"Why is January?"

All of a sudden, there is new light in Milton's eyes. The wheels are turning again.

"I have no idea," he says. "But I say we find out."

I decide to get the ball rolling.

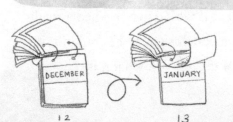

Why is January? . . . Let's see . . . because *some* month had to come first.

Yes. January is the *first* month of the year. But it's not *always* first. After all, it comes right *after* December.

I feel as if we've just reached a really important conclusion, but I couldn't for the life of me tell you what it is.

Was that helpful? I ask.

I'm not sure, says Milton.

Maybe... I say,

it means that even if you've always thought of someone as being good and sweet and nice, it's entirely possible that they are actually the most loathsome kind of owl thief.

Or maybe it means that even if all the evidence seems to point in one direction, there's another, completely different way of looking at things that will help you see the truth, says Milton.

This isn't working. We shouldn't be coming to

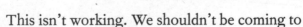

OPPOSITE CONCLUSIONS.

Maybe we just need to try again. Or maybe Annabelle was wrong and you really *can't* use someone's own diabolical problem-solving technique against her.

MY BAD.

I'm still trying to sort it out when the bell rings, ending second recess and leaving us no closer than we were before to figuring out where Eddie is now.

I look to Milton for some sort of insight, but, apparently, he doesn't have anything else to say. He wanders slowly back to the first-grade line, his mind in another place. We fourth graders pick up our piñatas and get ready to go back inside.

I watch as Emily stands there with her Earth piñata. She doesn't look good—even more tired and sweaty than before. I'm trying to figure out what in the world she might be thinking, but it's very hard to concentrate because Tracy Dublinger is twirling around like a crazy top, holding her molar piñata in one hand and Tammy's Tracy Dublinger piñata in her other hand while Tammy shrieks at her to cut it out. It's a delicious moment of Dublinger disagreement, and I'm enjoying it immensely.

218

But just then Tracy lunges crazily—and purposefully?—in my direction, and her huge molar crashes right into the back of my head. **OW!** I say, and then immediately wish I hadn't, because it doesn't actually hurt at all. As it turns out, a tooth made out of newspaper and glue doesn't pack much punch.

"Watch where you're going, *Moxie*," says Tracy.

I try to ignore her—in the way one tries to ignore the itch of poison ivy.

How I wish that Tracy were the crook! If I were a different kind of person, I'd figure out a way to frame her, but that is not my style.

Instead I decide to be as patient and wise as I possibly can. I let Tracy pretend that she didn't mean to hit me with her tooth. I let her believe that she has the upper hand. I will have the last laugh eventually.

I move to the back of the line, keeping my eye on Tracy Dublinger until she slips into the bathroom across the hall from the first-grade classroom.

I glance over, and there is Milton sitting at his desk in the last row. I give him a little wave, and he waves back, but it's clear that his mind is somewhere else.

When I get back to my desk, my graded spelling test is waiting. I got a zero out of ten, which is a complete and total outrage! Clearly, Mrs. Bunyan has *no idea* how to spell Rick's name!

Lucky for her, I have bigger problems at the moment. I need to figure out where Eddie is before the day ends and Milton gets carted off to jail and the real thief escapes on a speedboat bound for a renegade nation that refuses to return kidnapped mascots.

Even though every shred of evidence points to Emily,

I'm still trying to keep an open mind—in part because Principal Jones asked me to and in part because it pains me to think my leading best friend candidate could do such a thing. I need to figure out once and for all whether Emily is capable of such an awful act.

Since I missed the chance to interrogate her in person during second recess, I decide to do the next best thing.

Mrs. Bunyan has asked us to write five-paragraph essays on the spirit of the holiday, and so, for the first time all day, I actually sort of halfway do what I am supposed to.

I take out a piece of paper and write,

You sure look nice today.

I sign my name and fold the paper into the shape of a ninja throwing star (a trick I learned from a fifth grader named Phil) and toss it over onto Emily's desk, which is two desks to my right.

It barely misses the jutting chin of Chaz Danson, who sits between us, and hits Emily in the shoulder, which startles her at first. But then she opens it and reads my note.

I keep one eye on Mrs. Bunyan, who is sitting at her desk, scribbling on a piece of paper. Is she writing a holiday essay, too? Or a grocery list? Or maybe another list of awful words for my next spelling test?

Emily takes out her pen and writes something down.

At first she tries to fold the note back into a throwing star but then gives up and just mashes it into a crumpled blob and hands it to Chaz.

Chaz hands it over to me even though it's clear he doesn't want to.

I read Emily's note. It says,

you sure loo...

Thanks. That's nice of you to say.

Clearly, I have her right where I want her.

No problem, I write back.
You must get up really early to
make yourself look so fabulous.

I hand the note to Chaz. He
rolls his eyes. But then I give him
a Wallaby Death Stare, courtesy
of Annabelle Adams in

Volume 36: **Way Down Under,**

and he falls into line.

I read Emily's reply.

Actually, I got up LATE this morning.
And I think I look AWFUL.

I need to get this moving. Every time we pass the note,
we risk getting caught. And I haven't even gotten to the
most important questions yet.

So you fell asleep on the bus this morning. That's pretty weird.

Right? I can't believe it!

Has that ever happened to you before?

Nope. I think I'm a little sick.

Then why did you come to school today?

I didn't want to miss the assembly. It's my favorite day of the year.

I know, right? The awards are so exciting.

There's almost nothing better, except for maybe slugs after a rainstorm.

Excuse me. What did you say?

Slugs. I love them. ♡

Are you pulling my leg?

I know they are slimy and all, but I just can't get enough of their cute little antennae.

I know! I love their antennae!

At this point, Chaz has completely given up trying to resist. He is doing what I say because he fears the consequences if he doesn't. The Death Stare is surprisingly effective.

I have a terrarium full of them at home.
Seriously?!
Seriously. Do you want to come over and see them sometime?

I am about to write back **YES!!** and am planning to underline it twice and circle it three times, when I suddenly see what Emily is up to.

In Volume 21: **Tasting Her Own Medicine,**

Annabelle goes undercover as a geologist and makes friends with an influential oil tycoon named Jeremy—only to discover that Jeremy is *actually* her nemesis, Dr. Fungo, who has gone even *deeper* undercover to fool her.

Annabelle did her best to prepare me for this very moment! How could I have let myself be tricked? Somehow, Emily has discovered my weakness for slugs and is using it against me! I change from my blue pen to my black pen and get back to business.

Did you make any stops between the bus and our classroom?
Let's see... I stopped at the front desk to check in and get a hall pass.
Any other stops?
Nope. Why do you ask?

I glance over at Emily. She looks confused, as if someone has just changed the channel in the middle of her favorite TV show.

She knows I have found her out. The guilt is seeping in.

It's extremely important that you tell the complete truth. People who lie about what they do on the way to school in the morning can end up in prison for up to seven years. It's in the Constitution.
Is that true?

Emily is looking sweatier by the minute. I can tell Chaz is about to lose his patience. I give him a peppermint.

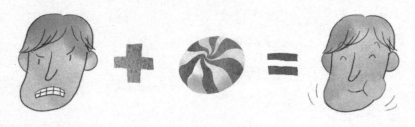

Absolutely. Have you ever seen a movie about lawyers?
No. My dads don't let me go to movies.
The jails don't even have bathrooms. You just have to hold it. So where else did you stop? Think carefully.

I guess I stopped in the pink bathroom. I really had to pee.

AND WHY DIDN'T YOU MENTION THIS BEFORE?

I use really big letters to rattle her.

It didn't seem important.

This is classic criminal behavior! Dodging my questions. Conveniently forgetting critical details! I am getting under Emily's skin. Soon the truth will be mine.

Do you have any witnesses who can confirm your version of the story?

I'm sorry. This has been super fun, but I have to throw up.

I glance over, and Emily gives me a friendly, apologetic smile. Somehow, she has managed to make her skin look a little bit green. I have to admit, I am impressed.

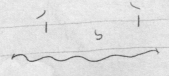

She raises her hand, and I panic. She is going to tell Mrs. Bunyan that I have been interrogating her. I just need a few more minutes to put it all together.

I'm not feeling very good, says Emily.

I need to go to the nurse's office.

As Emily takes her hall pass and leaves the room, my mind is scrambling to make sense of what she has just told me.

The two sets of bathrooms at Tiddlywhump are different colors so that teachers can send you to a specific one. A few years ago, a kindergartner named Molly Blip would always go to the bathroom on the other side of the school instead of the one that was closest to her classroom. One time she got lost and cried so much that her shirt got really wet.

After that, they painted the bathrooms specific colors
that relate to the colors of your hall pass. Sixth graders
(yellow), fifth graders (blue), and fourth graders (green) use
the green bathrooms. (Because yellow and blue make green.)

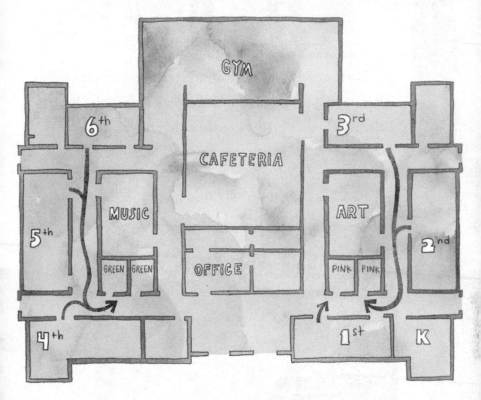

And third graders (white), second graders (red), first
graders (pink), and kindergartners (white with a red stripe)
use the pink bathrooms. (Because white and red make pink.)
Confusing? *Only at first.* A good way to teach little kids how
colors work? *Absolutely.*

There were a few third-grade boys who made a stink, saying they wouldn't use a pink bathroom. But Principal Jones said they could either hold it all day long or grow up to be more open-minded men.

Ever since the Molly Blip incident,

MOLLY BLIP INCIDENT

BREAKING NEWS

MISSING CHILD
REPORTED FOUND
CRYING IN CLOSET

if you're caught in the wrong bathroom, you lose an Owl Point.

SEEMS FAIR TO ME.

Suddenly, everything is perfectly clear.

It would be the *perfect* place to stash a stolen owl.

CHAPTER 11: McCOYS UNITE

I raise my hand and tell Mrs. Bunyan that I need to go to the bathroom, and you can tell that letting me go hurts about as much as sticking a fork in her eye, but I get my hall pass and leave the classroom. I have a problem:

Fourth graders are supposed to use the *green* bathrooms.

And I need to get to the *pink* bathrooms.

GREEN

PINK

Which means this will be a risky operation, but so is performing a double lung transplant to save a key witness right after a yearly eye exam when your pupils are still dilated as in   Volume 5: *Seeing Double,* and Annabelle did that on three hours of sleep and with an empty stomach. Which is to say, I am up to the challenge.

To reach the pink bathrooms, I need to walk through the front lobby. I can see Mrs. Breath typing away at her desk, too busy to notice me tiptoeing by. I make it past the big glass window and take a deep breath.

There is Eddie's case, empty and sad.

I slip into the girls' pink bathroom and look around. There just aren't many places where you could hide an owl of Eddie's size and magnificence. I check under all the sinks. *Nothing.* I look behind all the toilets. *No Eddie.*

A horrible thought occurs to me, and I check inside the trash can. Fortunately, it is mostly empty, except for a few paper towels and a lollipop stick. On a normal day, I would immediately start trying to figure out who has eaten a lollipop, which is forbidden at Tiddlywhump Elementary.

But this is not a normal day.

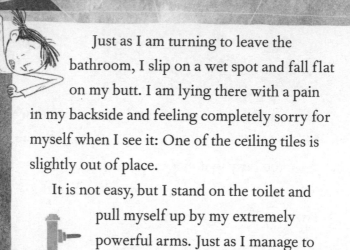

Just as I am turning to leave the bathroom, I slip on a wet spot and fall flat on my butt. I am lying there with a pain in my backside and feeling completely sorry for myself when I see it: One of the ceiling tiles is slightly out of place.

It is not easy, but I stand on the toilet and pull myself up by my extremely powerful arms. Just as I manage to wedge myself into the space between the top of the stall and the ceiling, I hear someone come in.

I have a moment of absolute panic, fearing that it is Principal Jones or Mrs. Breath or a cold-blooded killer with a chain saw. But when I turn and look, it is just a kindergartner named BethAnn.

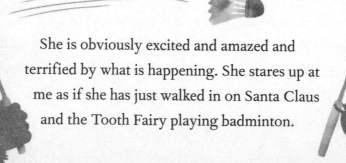

She is obviously excited and amazed and terrified by what is happening. She stares up at me as if she has just walked in on Santa Claus and the Tooth Fairy playing badminton.

Which must be upsetting to her, because she opens her mouth as if she's going to scream.

 I am in your imagination. Really?

 Really.

This seems to make her feel much better.

 Oh. Can you walk through walls?

 Yes, that's how I got in here. That's funny.

 Thank you.

BethAnn does what she has to do. Then she washes her hands.

 Good-bye. See you later.

I can tell she's a little bit worried again.

 BethAnn. What?

 Don't tell anyone you saw me. Okay.

I figure I'd better hurry in case BethAnn does not keep her word. I inch myself over to the loose tile and push it up with my nose. I peer into the darkness, which is full of dust, which gets in my nose and eyes and almost makes me lose my balance.

Almost.

I blink a lot, and my nose runs a little, but in the darkness, I see something that doesn't quite belong: a handsome blue monocle.

Eddie was here! Right where Emily admitted to being around the time he was stolen! But how do I *prove* she put him here? And where is he *now*? Just telling Principal Jones about Emily isn't going to be enough. It's clear she isn't going to accept anything less than the bird in her hands.

I grab the monocle and climb back down. There's no time for pride. I need to crack this case, and I can't do it on my own.

I need Maude, but she's not here.

I need the best friend candidate version of Emily Estevez, but instead I am stuck with the deranged criminal version.

Which means, and I hate to admit it, but as I learned from Volume 39: *They Call for Desperate Measures*, in which Annabelle drapes eleven poisonous variable coral snakes across her head, neck, and shoulders to convince a nearsighted sultan that she actually is an obscure Mayan goddess, this is a desperate time.

There are no other options. I need Milton.

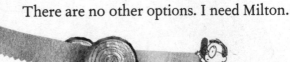

FIRST-GRADE
CLASSROOM

Fortunately, the first-grade classroom
is right across the hallway from the pink
bathrooms. I crouch outside the door and
peek in through the window. There is Milton
in the back row, writing in his notebook.

I have to figure out
how to get his attention, but
I don't see any way to do it without
getting everyone else's attention, too.
So I wait. And wait. Eventually, a kid
comes out. His name is John. He is as
skinny as a piece of paper. I have seen
him get startled by leaves falling
out of trees.

I try not to scare him, but I do.
He yelps a little when he sees me.

Don't hurt me!

I'm not going to hurt you, John.

Thank you. I'm just a first grader.

I know, John. You just came out of the FIRST-GRADE CLASSROOM.

John glances at the sign on the door, just to make sure that what I've said is true.

I'm Milton's sister.

I know who you are from

Don't hurt me!

We've been over this. I'm not going to hurt you. I just need you to do me a favor.

Here! he says, reaching into his pocket and pulling out a dollar.

Put away your dollar, John.

Okay, he says. He is kind of panting and seems to be turning purple.

I am considering all the fun things I could ask John to do.

Jump on one leg.

Or meow like a kitten.

But I'm running out of time, so I decide to stick to the basics. I tear a page out of my notebook and write a message to Milton.

I NEED YOUR HELP. GET OUT OF CLASS HOWEVER YOU CAN. IT IS AN EMERGENCY.

"Now take this note to Milton," I say.

"Okay," says John, lunging for the classroom door.

"John," I say.

"Yes?" he says, turning kind of yellow this time.

"Be sneaky about it. Don't let Mr. Brightenhouse see."

"Okay," he says. "I'll try."

I look John straight in the eye, using Annabelle Adams's advanced brain wave–amplification technique (from Volume 11: *Move Over, Einstein*) to make him calm and confident.

"Don't *try*, John. Just do," I say. I blink three times, which is an important part of the technique.

John looks as if he might actually cry.

"Go," I say. He goes. He's walking kind of funny, and I realize that he was probably on his way to the bathroom before I interrupted his mission.

I watch as John walks across the room and hands the note to Milton. It is perhaps the least stealthy delivery of a top secret note that I have ever seen in my entire life.

Fortunately, Mr. Brightenhouse doesn't seem to notice. He is busy trying to explain which is why Milton isn't paying attention, because he has known how to add and subtract since he was four years old.

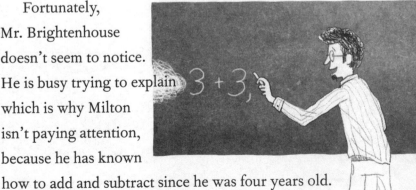

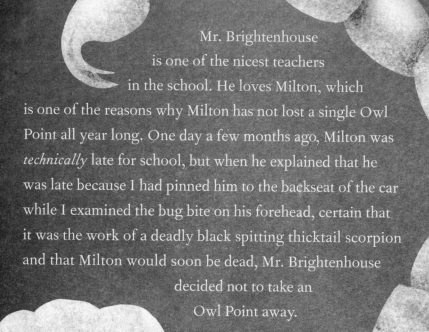

Mr. Brightenhouse
is one of the nicest teachers
in the school. He loves Milton, which
is one of the reasons why Milton has not lost a single Owl
Point all year long. One day a few months ago, Milton was
technically late for school, but when he explained that he
was late because I had pinned him to the backseat of the car
while I examined the bug bite on his forehead, certain that
it was the work of a deadly black spitting thicktail scorpion
and that Milton would soon be dead, Mr. Brightenhouse
decided not to take an
Owl Point away.

It turned out that it was just a mosquito bite, but MY BAD!
the point is that I might have saved my brother's life.

I can see Milton sitting there, reading my note and not knowing what to do. At a certain point, he connects the dots and looks over at the door.

When he sees me peeking through the window, he gives me a look that seems to mean,

Even though it makes me incredibly sad to lie and tell Mr. Brightenhouse that I have to go to the bathroom when I don't actually have to go to the bathroom, I am going to do what

you are asking because I know it's important and I would do anything for you because you are the greatest sister in the world and you need me in this desperate moment.

I watch as Milton raises his hand and gets a hall pass and comes out into the hallway.

What do you want?

I *know* Emily did it.

You don't know for sure.

I do, in fact.

Why do you have it in for Emily?

I don't!

And I actually mean it. I'm deeply disappointed that the Emily I thought I knew is no longer in the running to be my new best friend. "If I have it in for anyone, it's that horrible Tracy Dublinger. She knocked me in the head with her gigantic molar at the end of second recess, almost 100% certainly on purpose."

Are you okay?

Milton seems genuinely concerned.

It didn't hurt at all. Piñatas are extremely hollow. My head is extremely hard.

That's true enough,

says Milton,
who looks like he is
thinking about something.

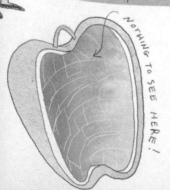

NOTHING TO SEE HERE!

CHEEP! CHEEP!

To keep things moving, I pull Eddie's monocle out of my pocket. Milton's eyes get wide. He takes the monocle and cradles it in his hands as if it were a baby bird that just fell out of its nest.

"Where did you find this?" Milton asks.

"Above a loose tile in the ceiling of the girls' pink bathroom."

"What makes you think *Emily* put him up there?"

"She admitted that she stopped by the pink bathroom on the way to class this morning."

"Lots of people have been in that bathroom today."

"But Emily is a *fourth grader* who would have been carrying a *green hall pass*."

247

And what about the greasy thumbprint?

asks Milton.

I had forgotten all about the thumbprint. I'm trying to figure out if there is any reason why Emily might have had greasy thumbs today. Maybe because she's been so sweaty?

But it hardly matters. Because I have the *physical evidence*. The monocle. *Right where Emily had said she was at the exact time Eddie was stolen.*

This is the smoking gun,

I tell Milton.

Annabelle Adams is always talking about the smoking gun. I guess guns with smoke coming out of them are often important clues in solving crimes, even when the crime itself was committed with nunchucks or a spatula, which seems a little weird, but there you go.

"But why would Emily do it?" asks Milton, shaking his head.

Milton is right to consider Emily's motive, but I'm one step ahead of him.

"Emily knew that, because I am so great, she probably wasn't going to win the Eddie Award this time, and so she tried to sabotage the whole thing."

It's possible that she's even planning on returning Eddie to Principal Jones to make herself look like a hero.

Or maybe she's going to do something terrible to Eddie so that no one can ever win the Eddie Award again.

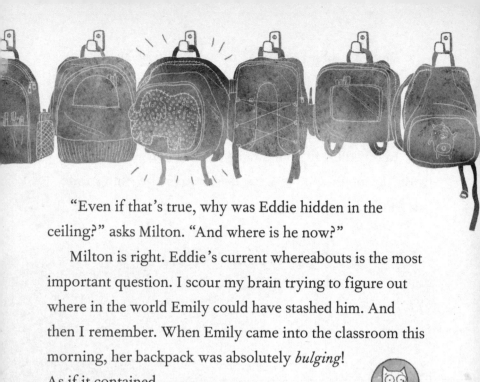

"Even if that's true, why was Eddie hidden in the ceiling?" asks Milton. "And where is he now?"

Milton is right. Eddie's current whereabouts is the most important question. I scour my brain trying to figure out where in the world Emily could have stashed him. And then I remember. When Emily came into the classroom this morning, her backpack was absolutely *bulging*! As if it contained . . .

I tell Milton about the backpack. "Maybe she stole Eddie, put him in the ceiling, changed her mind, and put him in her backpack without realizing that she'd lost the monocle," I say.

"That doesn't add up," says Milton. "I just need a minute to think."

+

———

O

"We don't have a minute," I say. "Emily is already at the nurse's office. I've got to tell Principal Jones about Emily before Nurse Crockett sends her home!"

"Principal Jones said you had to be *sure*," says Milton.

"I'm sure *enough*."

Milton looks at me like he wants to say something and also *doesn't* want to say it. But then he says it anyway.

You may be brave. And also pretty wise. But sometimes you're not very patient.

I feel like Milton has just hit me in the head with something a lot heavier than a piñata, and I consider saying something in return.

But instead I decide to "turn the other cheek."

Apparently, when someone says something horrible to you and you turn your head in the opposite direction instead of saying something even more horrible to them, they will sometimes feel bad and apologize.

I turn my head the other way and say,

You're very sweet, Milton, but you're just a kid. You are not in fourth grade. You do not understand the vast mysteries of the world. And you do not have a bug named after you.

Milton looks at me for a long time.

"Actually, I *do* have a bug named after me."

"No, you don't," I say. Because, of course, he doesn't.

"I didn't tell you, because I didn't want to hurt your feelings," he says. "Mom told me about it a few weeks ago. It's called the MILTOMAJORUS. And it has an orange butt."

Just when I thought the day couldn't get any worse, I find out that I am not the only person in school with a bug named after her. I am not even the only person in my *family* with a bug named after her.

The world as I know it comes crashing down. This is not the kind of news that a person likes to hear in the middle of the most important case of her whole entire life.

Milton and I look at each other. Neither one of us knows what to say. I can tell he kind of wants to say he's sorry but also doesn't want to.

And he can tell I kind of
want to tell him that it's okay
but also kind of don't.

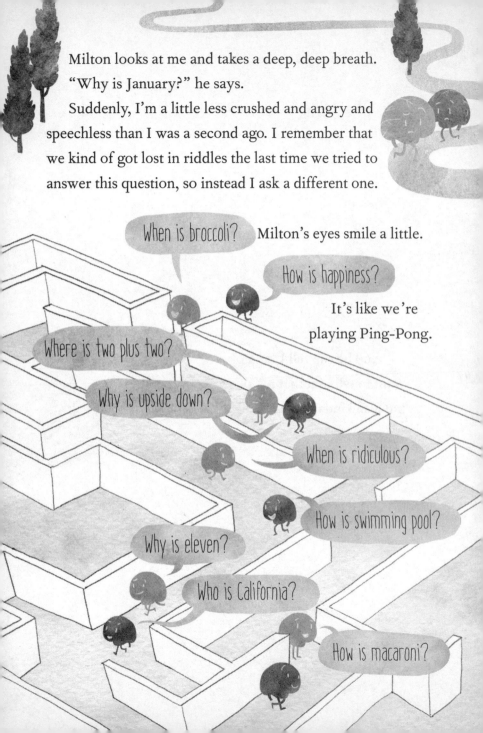

Milton looks at me and takes a deep, deep breath. "Why is January?" he says.

Suddenly, I'm a little less crushed and angry and speechless than I was a second ago. I remember that we kind of got lost in riddles the last time we tried to answer this question, so instead I ask a different one.

When is broccoli? Milton's eyes smile a little.

How is happiness?

It's like we're playing Ping-Pong.

Where is two plus two?

Why is upside down?

When is ridiculous?

How is swimming pool?

Why is eleven?

Who is California?

How is macaroni?

When is . . . Mom coming home?

Milton's face changes as the fun goes out of the game.

Where is . . .

And then my brain registers what Milton just said and is suddenly quite *un*stuck and ready to get back to the matter at hand.

. . . Emily's backpack now?

says Milton, without missing a beat.

We snap back to detective mode. I want to give Milton a high five. But there's no time.

It's in Mrs. Bunyan's classroom.

And where is Emily?

In the nurse's office.

Are you sure?

There's only one way to find out.

I look down the hallway toward the main office. If we peek through the big glass window, we should be able to see what's happening in the nurse's office.

Milton looks at me and down at his hall pass and then back at me.

I know what he's thinking. His hall pass only lets him walk between his classroom and the pink bathrooms. If he gets caught over by the main office, he's  TOAST.

"I'll do it," I say. "You go back to class. I'll let you know what happens."

Milton looks at me and holds out his tiny hand. I'm not sure what to make of it, but then I realize he wants to shake.

We're in this together,

he says.

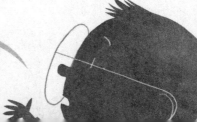

I look at Milton standing there. As small and as young and as falsely accused as he might be, he's never seemed braver. Eddie would be proud.

"All right," I say, taking his hand in mine. "Let's do it." The two of us creep down the hallway together and crawl on all fours when we get to the front office. I poke my head up and peek through the window.

Fortunately, Mrs. Breath is too busy murdering her keyboard to notice me. Off to the side, I see Emily on the bench outside the nurse's office looking miserable. I know that bench. It's where sick kids sit when they are waiting for their parents to come pick them up. It's where Maude and I cried about soup and became best friends.

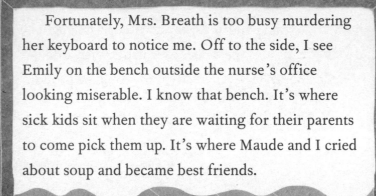

They're sending her home! I say.

This is our last chance!

How does she look?

Really sick, I say.

Pale, kind of greenish. She's a criminal mastermind.

Or maybe she's actually sick.

Impossible.

I want to see, says Milton.

I pop back down, and Milton pokes
his head up to get a better look at Emily.

"I don't think she's faking."

"She's faking," I say. "I *know* it."

"I'm not so sure," says Milton.

Uh-oh, he says, about an octave higher.

Uh-oh?

Oh man, he says. *I'm sorry.*

I have no idea what Milton is talking about, so I poke my
head up, too, and immediately wish I hadn't.

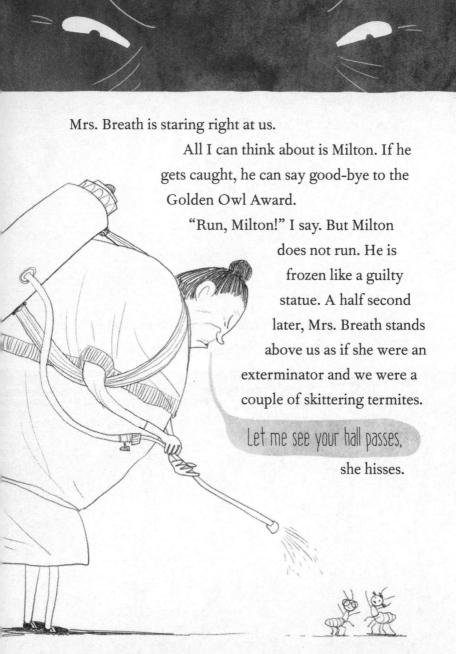

Mrs. Breath is staring right at us.

All I can think about is Milton. If he gets caught, he can say good-bye to the Golden Owl Award.

"Run, Milton!" I say. But Milton does not run. He is frozen like a guilty statue. A half second later, Mrs. Breath stands above us as if she were an exterminator and we were a couple of skittering termites.

Let me see your hall passes,

she hisses.

I hand her my green hall pass. Mrs. Breath takes one look at it and snarls. I can almost see a little bit of fire curling out of her nostrils. I am much farther away from the green bathrooms than I should be.

Milton hands over his pink hall pass. I can see in Milton's eyes what he is thinking. He's not *so* far away from the pink bathrooms. She could let him go if she really *wanted* to. Hope flickers in Milton's eyes.

But I know better.

That'll be one Owl Point from each of you,

says Mrs. Breath as cheerfully as if she had just won a pie-eating contest.

Milton's face falls, and so does my heart. To me, losing an Owl Point is like getting a mild sunburn— slightly unpleasant but not such a big deal. But to Milton, one Owl Point might as well be a hundred.

Mrs. Breath is so proud of herself that she looks like she might break into song. I can't think of anything more horrible.

 **You, get back to class,** she barks, looking right at me.

And, you, come with me, she says to Milton.

I watch as she leads him back toward the first-grade classroom. He looks so small. I can't imagine what he's thinking and feeling. All his hard work is suddenly lost. And it's all my fault.

I expect Milton to burst into tears or crumble into sand, but instead he turns around and looks at me.

THE BACKPACK... GO FIND EMILY'S BACKPACK!

"Stop talking!" says Mrs. Breath. "Be quiet!" You can tell that she's itching to take away more Owl Points.

"I'll find Eddie," I say. "I'll find him for *you*!"

Mrs. Breath steers Milton down the hallway to his classroom, and I hurry back toward mine.

The only thing I can do for Milton now is finish what we've started. I may not be able to get his Owl Point back, but maybe, just maybe, I can rescue the owl.

CHAPTER 12: THE TELLTALE BACKPACK

My heart is pounding when I get back to the classroom. I look over at the row of backpacks hanging along the wall and . . . Emily's is still there, stuffed so full that the poor zipper looks like it might give up at any second.

I want to go over and rescue Eddie right away, but I am on very thin ice with Mrs. Bunyan, who hasn't yet recovered from the hug. As I sit down at my desk, she gives me an awful look because, once again, I have been gone a really long time.

I get the sense she is deciding whether to send me straight back to Principal Jones, when Nurse Crockett comes in and tells her that Emily is sick and is heading home. She has come to collect Emily's things.

I panic. Only moments remain until Emily and her backpack and Eddie leave the school. If I don't act now, I will regret it forever.

Mrs. Bunyan and Nurse Crockett are deep in conversation about which local grocery store offers the  BEST *Holiday* SAVINGS.

> Acme, of course. Two for one this week on candy canes.

> Get out of town!

> I couldn't believe it myself.

> Tee. Hee. Hee.

Fortunately, Nurse Crockett has a funny way of laughing at the end of every sentence, so all the kids are focusing on how goofy she sounds.

Which gives me a chance to walk over to the pencil sharpener at the back of the classroom near the hooks where the backpacks hang. I stand there sharpening

REALLY LOUDLY

to let everyone know that my pencil is

GOOD AND DULL

and that it's going to take a long, long time to get it sharp again.

In the meantime, Mrs. Bunyan and Nurse Crockett move on to a rousing discussion of their favorite cookie recipes.

"Gingersnaps?"

"Nope."

"Almond crescents?"

"Getting colder."

"Snickerdoodles?"

"YES! *Snickerdoodles!* Tee. Hee. Hee."

Very slowly, inch by inch, I creep toward Emily's backpack. Somehow, incredibly, no one has noticed what I'm up to, and I cross my fingers that the hilarious show at the front of the room will keep going long enough for me to rescue Eddie.

Mrs. Bunyan and Nurse Crockett are now discussing where each of them will be spending the winter holidays.

With my folks in Jersey.

With my boyfriend in Tampa.

Amen, sister. Tee. Hee. Hee.

I figure that at some point they will remember that there is an actual human being waiting in the nurse's office. Which means that time is running out.

As I reach for the zipper, I don't know how to feel.

On one hand, I want to find Eddie inside—so that things can get back to how they were and so that Principal Jones can see that I'm amazing, too.

But on the other hand, finding Eddie in Emily's backpack would mean she'll never be the soup-hating, slug-loving new best friend of my dreams.

I want to open the backpack and I don't.

I want to have it both ways. *But I can't.*

While I have been thinking, the discussion at the front of the room has finally turned to Emily herself.

"Is she going to be okay?"

"She'll be fine. Just a little STOMACH BUG.

"I'm sure we both agree that she should brush her teeth before we send her home?"

"Well, I don't know if that's *absolutely* necessary. Tee. Hee. Hee."

They're winding down. It's now or never. I turn off my brain and shift into cold-blooded detective mode. I tug as hard as I can, but the backpack is so full that the zipper won't budge.

I tug and I tug.

I'm making the tiniest bit of progress when an unmistakable voice cuts through the air.

Whatcha doing, *Slim?*

It's Tracy Dublinger, saying my detective name for the first time in her life. She says it loud. *On-purpose* loud.

Mrs. Bunyan's head snaps up. "Get back to your seat this *instant*, Moxie McCoy!"

"But . . ." And I don't know what to say next. I'm moments from uncovering the truth, solving the mystery, and saving the day. All I need is a few more seconds. If I get sent to the principal's office before rescuing Eddie, all is lost!

"But *nothing*," says Mrs. Bunyan, grabbing the bowling pin off her desk and marching to the back of the room.

I tug with all my might. But the zipper stays stuck, and Mrs. Bunyan keeps coming.

Closer.

"I'm just . . . I'm just . . ." I am tugging at the zipper with every ounce of courage, patience, and wisdom I can muster.

And closer.

"I'm just bringing Emily's backpack to Nurse Crockett," I say between breaths. "I've got it . . . right . . . here. . . ."

And closer.

"Just . . . one . . . more . . . second . . ."

But like a bad cold you know is coming but can't seem to shake, suddenly Mrs. Bunyan is there.

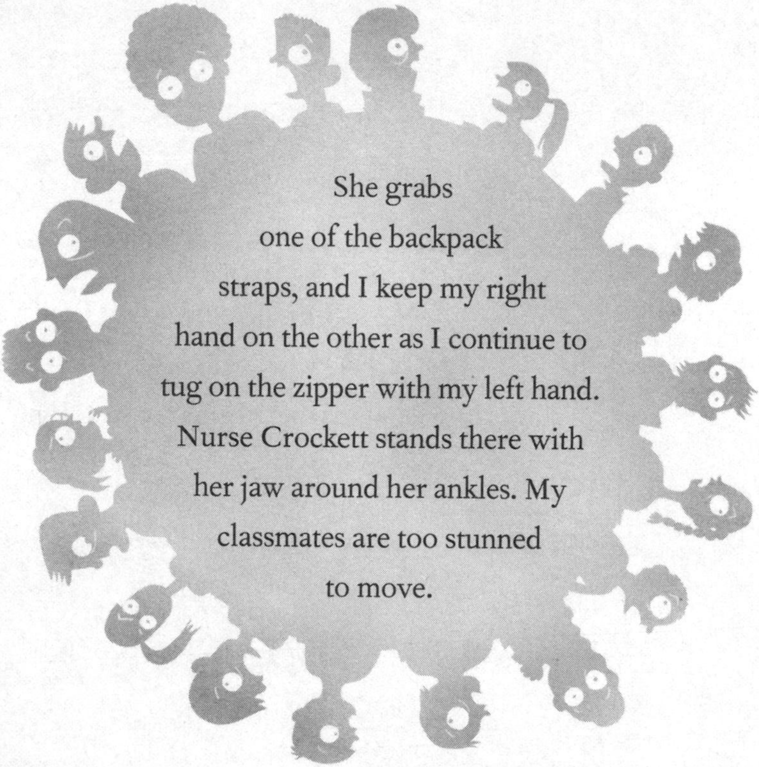

She grabs
one of the backpack
straps, and I keep my right
hand on the other as I continue to
tug on the zipper with my left hand.
Nurse Crockett stands there with
her jaw around her ankles. My
classmates are too stunned
to move.

Mrs. Bunyan and I are playing a mighty game of

TUG-OF-WAR,

both of us straining with all our might, neither one willing to
give an inch, when, finally, the zipper comes unstuck, *just a
bit*, and when it does,
I see *a little tuft of
brown fur inside!*

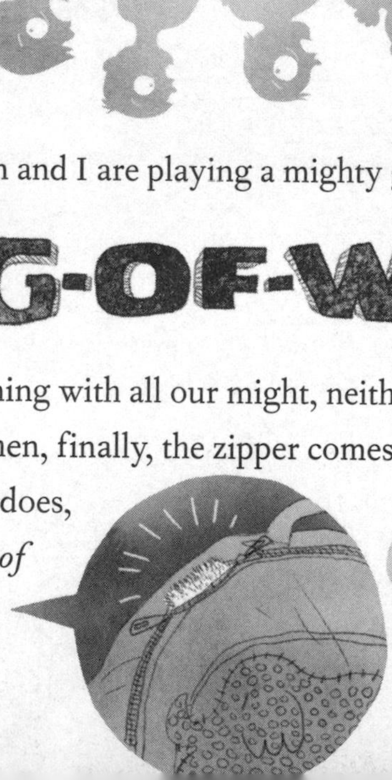

Eddie!

I say.

In my surprise, I let go of the backpack just enough that Mrs. Bunyan is able to wrestle it away from me. She hands it to Nurse Crockett, who scurries out the door as if the classroom were about to explode.

Which, in a way, it is.

Mrs. Bunyan looks at me like a hockey stick looks at a puck.

I'm pretty sure Mrs. Bunyan is not allowed to send me to the principal's office for the rest of the year, but it seems like the wrong moment to point this out.

I take a deep breath and grab the bowling pin. As I walk out of the classroom, I hear someone say,

I think her little brother might have stolen Eddie.

At first I can't tell who it was, but when I whip my head around, I see the beady eyes of my least favorite Dublinger staring at me. Of course, I want to go back and shove a sock into her smirking mouth, but it's clear that my last, best chance to clear Milton's name and save poor Eddie is escaping quickly down the hallway in Emily's backpack.

And so I take a deep breath and head for the main office. I will deal with Tracy later.

As I walk down the hall, I'm surprisingly nervous. On one hand, Principal Jones told me that I was not, under any circumstances, to keep looking for the crook. But technically, Eddie is a "missing person."

And so, of course, I have to let her know that he has been found.

And, of course, she has to forgive me.

Right?

I am pretty sure that this is how things work, but I can't remember any situation quite like this in any of Annabelle Adams's adventures. And so, for the first time all day, I'm not exactly sure what to do.

Somehow, I have to give Principal Jones all the important information before she locks me in the dungeon with Mrs. Breath and her dictionary. I try to think of the best words to use, but all my best words seem to be missing.

I walk through the door of the main office for what feels like the hundredth time today.

You, says Mrs. Breath.

Her eyes are a snake's eyes, and I feel like a mouse that she's going to toy with for fifteen minutes or so before swallowing in a single gulp and slowly digesting over a two- to three-week span. She sees the bowling pin and smiles with a wicked delight and presses the button on her phone.

Moxie McCoy, she says.

There is a long sigh and then

Send her in.

It is the voice of an evil robot overlord from the kind of movie kids aren't supposed to see.

I wonder if maybe the best thing is to run. I am fast enough to avoid being caught. I could take a new name and live in another country, maybe Guatemala. I've learned enough Spanish from Mom that I would be able to order lunch and ask where the bathroom is.

Quiero dos tacos, y ¿dónde está el baño?

But then I think about *my innocent brother in handcuffs* *and poor stolen Eddie* crammed into a backpack that is, at this very moment, about to be taken out of the school, into the wide world, so that two-faced Emily Estevez can do who knows what to him.

Milton needs me. Eddie needs me. My school needs me. Running away wouldn't help anyone but myself.

I take a deep breath. I put my hand on the knob and turn it.

Principal Jones,

I say.

I'm afraid you've run out of chances, Moxie.

From the look on Principal Jones's face, I get the sense that I'll have the opportunity to say just one thing before she pulls the lever that operates the trapdoor. I can either tell her who *did* steal

Eddie or I can tell her who *didn't*. The choice seems clear.

MILTON IS NOT AN OWL THIEF!

I say, louder than I'd intended.

I'm afraid I can't discuss this with you, Moxie,

says Principal Jones.

BUT HE'S *INNOCENT!*

How can you know that for sure?

Because he'd never, ever, ever do something like that. He is honest and loyal and true. He is the absolute best! You have to believe me.

280

The way Principal Jones is looking at me, I'm pretty sure she does.

But I can't take any chances.

"And because I figured out who *did* steal Eddie. I know where he is! At this very minute!"

Principal Jones sits up straight in her chair and looks so deeply into my eyes that I feel like I'm not wearing any clothes.

"This had better not be another false accusation."

"It's not. I swear. I *saw* him!"

"You saw who?

"I saw *Eddie*!" I say. I can tell our friendship is really getting back on track.

"With your *own eyes*?" she says. She is looking at me as if I were the last dose of medicine that will save her dying grandmother.

Yes!

I say.

Yes!

I pull out the monocle and hand it to Principal Jones. She gasps as if she has just discovered life on Mars.

"Where is the rest of him?" says Principal Jones.

"In Emily Estevez's backpack," I say. "But Emily is about to leave the school! She's pretending to be sick, and Nurse Crockett just sent her home. We don't have a moment to lose!"

Principal Jones pushes one of the buttons on her phone.

"Is Emily Estevez still there?" she says.

I hear Nurse Crockett's voice on the other end. "She just left my office."

Principal Jones stands up. "Come with me," she says. I honestly can't tell if she is getting ready to give me a prize or throw me in jail.

I follow her past Mrs. Breath's desk and into the lobby. There, about to leave through the front door, is Emily Estevez, holding on to her backpack like it's her only friend in the world.

Emily, please wait,

says Principal Jones.

Emily spins around, clearly terrified. She knows she's
been caught. I'm almost afraid to see
what happens next.

You're not in trouble, Emily.

Not yet,

I think.

May I look inside your backpack?

Sure,

says Emily.

Thank you.

As Principal Jones takes the backpack, I'm nervous and
excited and sad all at once. I'd had such high hopes for Emily.
Principal Jones pulls on the zipper,

and out pops . . .

. . . the unmistakable brown fuzzy fur of . . . Mr. Snuggles . . . a fuzzy brown pillow with a pink nose, googly eyes, and bushy bear ears. I've seen the commercial on TV. The jingle plays in my head . . .

Oh, Mr. Snuggles, what are we seeing?
A pillow, a bear, or an alien being?
A fuzzy potato with shiny pink shoes on?
One thing's for sure, you're a friend we can snooze on.

. . . as my mind splits neatly in two.

I am totally relieved and utterly crushed at the very same moment.

"Is this a pillow, Emily?" asks Principal Jones.

"Yes," says Emily, about to cry. "I wasn't feeling well this morning, so I brought Mr. Snuggles so I could take a nap on the bus. Is it against the rules to have a pillow in school?"

"Not at all," says Principal Jones, zipping the backpack up and handing it to Emily.

Can I go?

asks Emily.

I don't feel very good.

Of course,

says Principal Jones in the kindest voice I've ever heard in my entire life. I hardly recognize her. She pats Emily on the shoulder.

Emily is about to leave,
but I can't just let her go
without saying something, and
so I say a few words I don't
use very often.

"I'm sorry, Emily. I
never should have doubted
you. I was only trying to
save Eddie."

Emily looks at me with her
big, full heart, and I can tell
she knows I mean it.

"That's okay," she says.
"It's been a superweird day."

"It really has," I say.
"I'm going home now. See you
soon, I hope."

"Feel better," I say.

"Thanks."

"Wait, one more thing
before you go."

"Yeah?" says Emily.

"Can you by any chance shoot a bottle with a slingshot from 50 paces?"

"I don't think so," says Emily, smiling. "Does it matter?"

I look at her standing there, smiling at me in spite of all I've done to her today, and realize the answer to her question is not what I thought it would be.

"Nope. It doesn't matter at all."

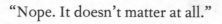

Emily's smile gets bigger and then her eyes get wide and then she turns green and says as politely as a butler offering someone a cucumber sandwich, "I'm sorry but I have to throw up again," before rushing out the door.

There goes my new best friend, I think, feeling happier than I've felt in a really long time—before remembering that I'm about to feel sadder than I've ever been in my whole entire life.

I turn around, and Principal Jones is looking at me with the eyes of a volcano that has been waiting about 500 years to erupt and has decided it's finally time. I am probably going to be kicked out of school and sent to live on a distant archipelago where I will have to survive on coconuts and kelp.

It's clear that Principal Jones is trying to figure out the quickest possible way to get me there, when I hear a voice that is both entirely familiar and completely unexpected.

STOP HER! STOP THAT OWL THIEF!!

It is Milton.

He is yelling at the top of his lungs and running toward us as quickly as he can, pointing wildly toward the front door of the school.

CHAPTER 13: THE OWL THIEF

Principal Jones and I look out
the window, but Emily is
already gone.

Not Emily,

says Milton, pointing behind us.

HER!

Principal Jones and I both turn to look. Milton is
pointing at someone else who is about to leave
through the door on the other side of
the lobby. It's Tracy Dublinger
and her gigantic molar,
presumably on
their way
to the
dentist.

At this point, it's clear that Principal Jones is entirely fed up with everyone in the McCoy family and that she's not interested in accusing anyone else of stealing Eddie, especially not the likely winner of the Wise Owl Award.

Tracy, would you please come here for a minute?

she says.

Tracy looks a little bit irritated but comes over anyway. After all, following directions is basically her favorite thing in the world.

Now,

says Principal Jones, looking at Milton,

why are you accusing Tracy Dublinger of stealing Eddie?

Because she did.

Could you be more specific?

Sure.

"Right after school started this morning, Tracy pretended that she had to go to the nurse's office to floss her teeth. Or maybe she actually *did* go see Nurse Crockett. That doesn't matter. What *does* matter is that, on the way, she grabbed Eddie from his case. But then she had to run into the pink bathroom when she heard Mr. Hammer whistling a tune as he came up the hall, which is why she knocked into the ropes and dropped the hall pass and left behind this long blond hair." As he says this, Milton walks over to the ropes around the case and picks up a long blond hair.

"That could belong to *anyone*!" says Tracy. "For example, it could be Tammy's." Tracy is glaring at Milton as if he were a fly and she were a rolled-up piece of newspaper.

Milton doesn't seem to notice Tracy's interruption or the possibility that he might get squashed, because he keeps right on going.

Tracy's thumbs were greasy because she was handing out Wonder Scout cookie samples before school started,

says Milton,

which is why she left a greasy thumbprint on the door of Eddie's case when she grabbed him.

At that, Tracy stuffs her hands into her pockets. Principal Jones looks not quite convinced but also not quite *not* convinced.

Tammy *also* sold cookies all morning,

says Tracy.

Get to the point, Milton,

says Principal Jones.

"Eddie spent most of his day stuffed up above the drop ceiling in the girls' pink bathroom," says Milton. He pauses for a moment, obviously upset from thinking about Eddie's difficult day.

"Until . . ." And there Milton pauses for a moment. It seems he also understands the importance of a good flourish. "Until Tracy stopped by the pink bathroom with her piñata on the way back from second recess."

So what if I did? snaps Tracy.

Suddenly, I'm starting to understand. "The first-grade classroom is right across the hall from the pink bathrooms," I say. "And since Milton's desk is in the back of the room by the door, he can see everyone who goes in and out!"

"Precisely," says Milton.

Milton couldn't possibly have known it, but *precisely* is one of Annabelle Adams's favorite things to say. He is a natural detective!

Milton continues, "When Tracy bashed Moxie in the head with her molar piñata at the end of second recess, it didn't hurt a bit. Because empty piñatas are not heavy.

Which is why, when Tracy went *into* the pink bathroom on the way back to her classroom, she was holding her piñata with *one* hand. But when she came back *out*, she was holding it with *two* hands."

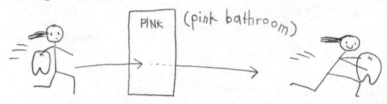

(pink bathroom)

"I'm not sure I understand what you're getting at," says Principal Jones.

We all look at Tracy. She is holding her molar piñata with two hands, but then she grabs onto it with just her right hand to show us how easy it is to hold with just one hand.

Only, it's *not* easy. It's obviously way too heavy to hold with just one hand. Because . . .

295

EDDIE IS HIDDEN INSIDE THE PIÑATA!

I say with the greatest flourish in the history of flourishes.

Is this true?

asks Principal Jones.

Tracy closes her eyes and looks like a sheep that just got sheared and is standing there naked and ashamed in front of all the other barnyard animals.

Every

last

word,

says Tracy, who is obviously not a criminal mastermind.

Principal Jones takes the piñata and gives it a shake. Thumping around inside is something that sounds unmistakably like a lovable owl with a missing monocle.

THUMP
THUMP!

Milton reaches over and lifts the top of the tooth, which opens with a cleverly built papier-mâché hinge.

I reluctantly admire Tracy Dublinger's remarkable attention to detail. If she ever gets out of jail, she might have a promising career as an engineer.

Milton hands Eddie to Principal Jones, who looks at Milton as if she were a grandma and he were a cheek she wants to pinch.

"How did you know all this?" she asks Milton. I can tell that she is rather impressed.

"From talking to Moxie," says Milton. "She had it figured out the whole time."

"You *did*?" asks Principal Jones, looking at me skeptically.

"Yes . . . *of course* . . . I did," I say, feeling happier about having Milton as a little brother than I ever have  in my entire life.

"Then why in the world did you accuse Bob and Leon and Emily?" asks Principal Jones.

I'm sitting there, trying to figure out what Annabelle Adams would say at a moment like this, when Milton says something instead.

We had to catch Tracy red-handed. And so we had to make her think we weren't onto her.

"I see," says Principal Jones, who seems not entirely convinced.

"What I can't figure out is *why* she did it," says Milton.

Milton makes an excellent point. What was Tracy's motive?

"Well?" says Principal Jones, looking right at Tracy.

Tracy looks like someone who has been trying to carry an anvil on her shoulder for a long, long time but really needs to set it down now. Her face goes from mad to sad to miserable to ashamed, and she bursts into tears.

"Why did you do it, Tracy?" asks Principal Jones.

"I wanted to *be wise like Eddie*," says Tracy between sobs. "I needed a *perfect score* on the spelling test to beat Tammy for the Wise Owl Award. I figured that if I kidnapped Eddie and gave him a really big hug, I'd get just a little bit of extra wisdom!"

"Did it work?" asks Milton.

"NO! I still spelled *amoeba* wrong! And Tammy got it *right*! We're supposed to be *identical*! It's

JUST...NOT...FAIR..."

I want to say something along the lines of, *Sorry, Tracy, but life's not always fair*. But it occurs to me that, in this very moment, it actually kind of is.

"I was going to put Eddie back, I swear!" she says, crying.

Then why did you put him inside the piñata?

asks Principal Jones, suddenly
angry as a bee whose hive has
been knocked out of a tree.

Why were you trying
to take him home?

I thought maybe if I spent winter break
with Eddie . . . . I'd be a better speller
than Tammy by the start of spring term.
I... JUST... WANT...
TO... BE...THE...
BEST!

At this point, Tracy is purple and hyperventilating, and
I'm considering letting her know that I'm not a very good
speller, either, but then I remember what I'm pretty sure I
heard Tracy say as I was leaving Mrs. Bunyan's classroom.

"Do you have the anonymous note that accused Milton of stealing Eddie?" I ask Principal Jones.

"I do," she says, pulling it out her pocket.

"Tracy left *this* on my desk earlier," I say, handing the note about my hair to Principal Jones. She holds the two notes side by side.

The handwriting is *exactly* the same.

"Why would you accuse Milton of stealing Eddie?" asks Principal Jones, now as angry as at least a hundred bees.

Tiffany Eiffenbach . . . is . . . my cousin, sobs Tracy.

I . . . was trying . . . to help her win . . . the Golden Owl Award.

I had always suspected that there was something a little bit off about Tiffany Eiffenbach.

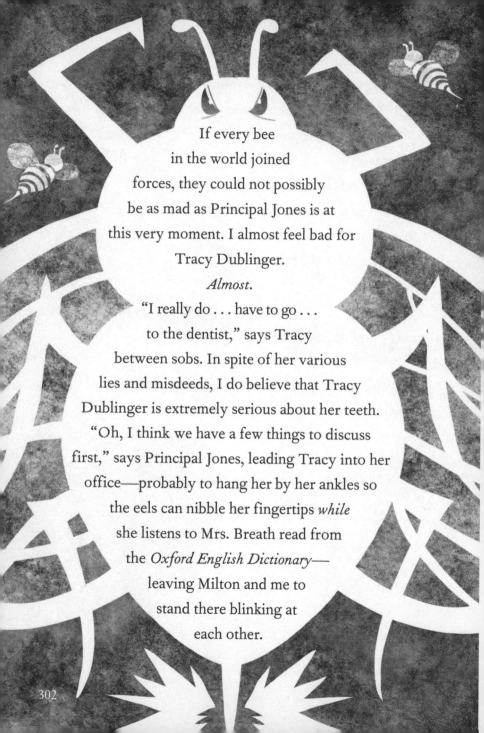

If every bee
in the world joined
forces, they could not possibly
be as mad as Principal Jones is at
this very moment. I almost feel bad for
Tracy Dublinger.

Almost.

"I really do . . . have to go . . .
to the dentist," says Tracy
between sobs. In spite of her various
lies and misdeeds, I do believe that Tracy
Dublinger is extremely serious about her teeth.

"Oh, I think we have a few things to discuss
first," says Principal Jones, leading Tracy into her
office—probably to hang her by her ankles so
the eels can nibble her fingertips *while*
she listens to Mrs. Breath read from
the *Oxford English Dictionary*—
leaving Milton and me to
stand there blinking at
each other.

"Thanks," I say. "Truly."

I should probably follow up with *You were right, Milton,* and *You're the best brother a sister could ask for* or other things like that, but I'm having trouble remembering how to pronounce those particular words.

So I give him a sort of hug, which is not really my style, and not really his style, either. But he gives me a sort of hug back, and then we're standing there together in the hallway again.

The one thing I can say is,

I'm really sorry about your Owl Point.

That's okay,

he says.

But it isn't. I'd do anything to get that Owl Point back.

"I'm just glad Eddie is okay," he says.

"Me too," I say. "We make a pretty good team, you know."

"You did all the hard work. I'm just glad I could help."

I take a long look at Milton. There's so much more to him than I ever realized. Inside that tiny body is an amazing human being and a respectable detective.

For the first time, I can see the possibility that he's my actual brother—that he's a *real* McCoy.

Milton holds out his hand, and I hold out mine. We have a good shake. After all, we did just solve the crime of the century.

As Milton heads back to his class, I let it all sink in. Eddie is back where he belongs. I have found my new best friend. And maybe even a new detective partner. Not bad for a day's work.

As I stand there wondering how life can possibly get better, I hear a buzz and a crackle and the voice of Principal Jones.

All students, please report to the auditorium for the assembly.

CHAPTER 14: THE ASSEMBLY

The assembly begins with the kindergartners singing "Jingle Bells." Listening to the mangled mess of it is like getting a thousand paper cuts all at once. Unfortunately, the awards happen at the *end* of the assembly.

We are next forced to watch as the first graders do a skit in which some of them are dressed like sheep and some are dressed like raisins. At least that's what it looks like.

I'm too busy preparing my Eddie Award acceptance speech to pay much attention to what's happening onstage. I am trying to decide whether I should thank the president of the United States and Annabelle Adams, when a hush falls over the crowd.

Principal Jones walks out onstage holding Eddie. A loud cheer fills the auditorium. We have never been so happy to see him.

"It has been a long and difficult day," says Principal Jones, "but Eddie is back where he belongs."

More cheering. Eddie is probably the most popular owl on the planet.

"And now we have some awards to hand out," says Principal Jones. More cheering. And then some more.

First up, the **Wise Owl Award,**

for the student who has best demonstrated Eddie's great wisdom. And the award goes to . . .

Principal Jones looks down at the piece of paper she is holding. I glance over at Tammy Dublinger, who is smoothing her hair and practicing her most horrible smile.

. . . Thomas Barlow,

says Principal Jones.

Tammy Dublinger's jaw drops like an apple falling from a tree. It's clear she can't decide whether to cry or yell or burst into flames.

Thomas, a great big sixth grader who could really use a haircut, walks up to the stage and shakes Principal Jones's hand. He is shocked and surprised, as if he has just discovered that he has an extra elbow. He takes his certificate and sits down.

I'm too busy feeling awful about the next award to properly enjoy the downfall of the Dublingers.

Next up, the Golden Owl Award,

says Principal Jones, for the student whose behavior is most in keeping with Eddie's fine example. And the winner is . . .

I look over at Milton. He's sitting there as quietly as an empty cicada shell. He has worked so hard for this award, and I messed it up for him.

All I can hope for is that somehow Tiffany Eiffenbach has *also* lost an Owl Point in the last hour or so.

But then Principal Jones says the exact two words I least want to hear.

Tiffany Eiffenbach.

There is a great flurry of cheering from a small group of second-grade girls who are clearly big Tiffany Eiffenbach fans. Tiffany bounces up onto the stage with an enthusiasm that would make Bob Tuttleman proud.

We all clap for Tiffany, but then the room goes silent. It's time for the Eddie Award. It feels like a spaceship has just landed in the middle of the auditorium and we're all waiting to see what kind of aliens are going to come out.

Principal Jones puts on her glasses. She takes an envelope out of her pocket.

And now to announce the winner of the Eddie Award, for the student who best embodies Eddie's courage, patience, and wisdom—a student who has gone to extraordinary lengths today to help this school *and* be a good sibling *and* show us the true meaning of selflessness, which isn't one of Eddie's virtues but probably should be.

My mental machine is going wild trying to figure out whether Principal Jones has just described me.

There's no denying I've helped Tiddlywhump today.

And how could one ask more of a sister than sharing top secret detective-training knowledge with her pint-sized little brother?

I am puzzling through what exactly Principal Jones means by "selflessness" when she says,

SHELFLESSNESS?

SHELLFISHNESS?

SHELFFISHNESS?

And the winner is . . .

Every student takes a breath all at once.

A full hour seems to pass before Principal Jones finishes her sentence.

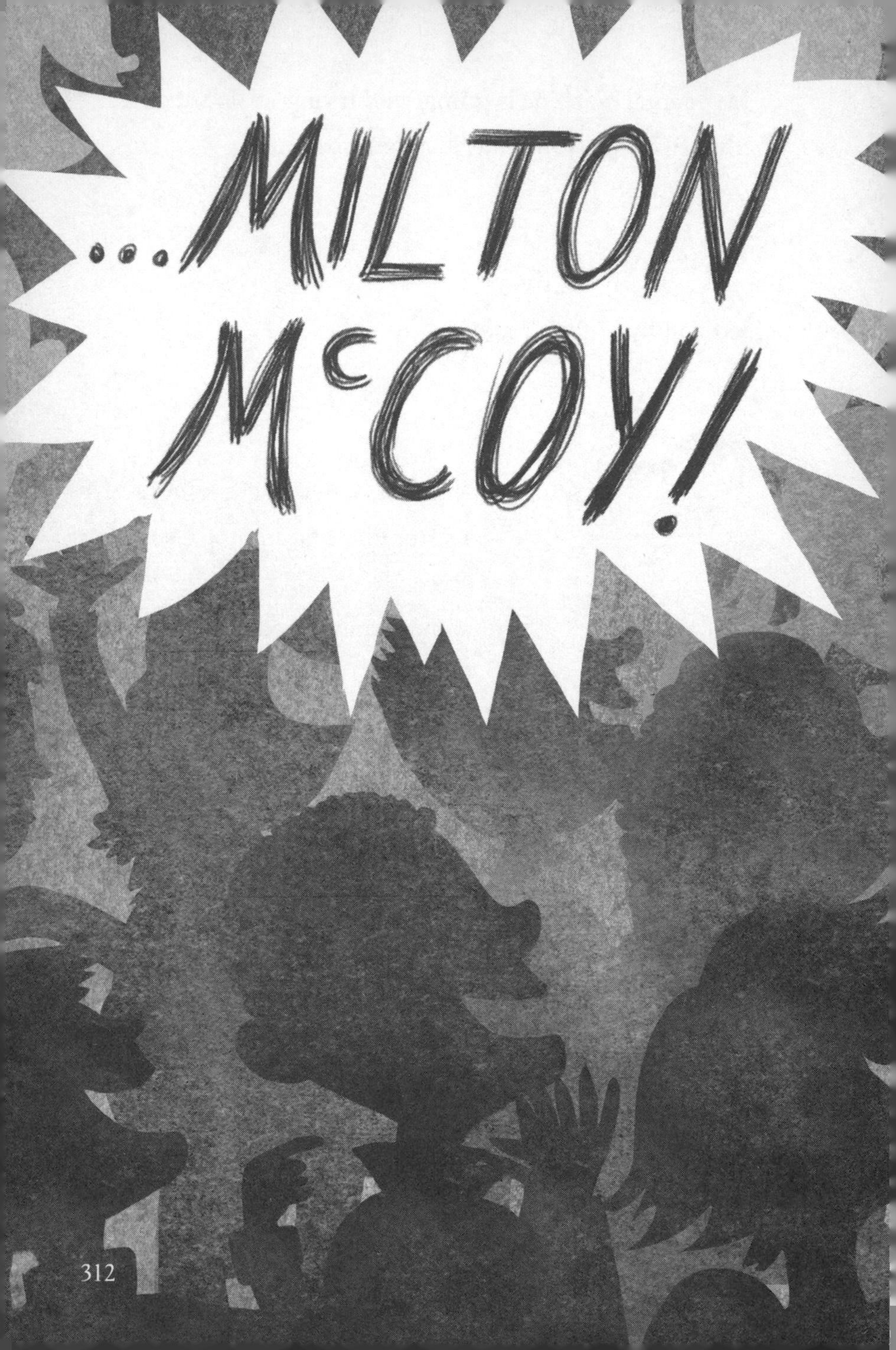
...MILTON McCOY!

I feel like a house that gets blown apart by a sudden tornado but then gets put back together again just a little bit better than it was before.

I look over at Milton. *Everyone* looks over at Milton. No first grader has ever won the Eddie Award. This is basically as shocking and exciting as the invention of the wheel. In an instant, Milton transforms from a piece of dry toast into a plate of happy lasagna. He sits straight up, and then he stands, and when he stands, various sixth-grade boys start chanting "Mil-*ton*! Mil-*ton*!"

I think they are doing it to be funny, but then other kids start saying it as well. "Mil-*ton*! Mil-*ton*! Mil-*ton*!"

I can't help but join in.

That's my little brother up there. And I taught him everything he knows.

This is very smart of Principal Jones, of course. Milton made important steps today in his development as a detective, and she wants to let him know he's on the right track.

There will be other problems that need solving in the future, and it will take *both* of us to get the job done.

Principal Jones and I both know that I am the real mastermind behind catching Tracy Dublinger. But sometimes it's even better to see something good happen to someone you love instead of getting it for yourself. Dad tells me this all the time, but I've never really understood it until this very moment.

CHAPTER 15: SERIOUSLY, WHY IS JANUARY?

After dinner that night, I call Mom and tell her about everything that happened today.

Wow,

she says.

Just your average day,

I say, though both of us know that's not quite true.

How's Milton?

Doing pretty good, I think.

How about you?

Never better.

It's only then that Mom tells me *her* news—just this morning she found the bug with the shiny green poop.

"Wow," I say.

"I'm going to call it Slim."

"I like that," I say. "Does this mean—"

"Yep," she says. "I'll be home the day after tomorrow."

I'd say something else, but I might be crying just a little.

"I love you," she says.

I say it back.

Before I go to bed, I go to my bookshelf and pull down a book I haven't read in a long time,

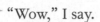

Volume 1:

Meet Annabelle Adams.

It's where Annabelle encounters her first mystery and discovers that she is a detective and makes a few mistakes along the way but catches the bad guy in the end. It's probably my favorite book in the entire world.

I carry it down the hall to Milton's room, but he's still in the bathroom brushing his teeth. I leave the book on his pillow and head back to my room. If we're going to join forces, he has some reading to do.

I sit by my window. Flurries are starting to fall. I pull out my notebook and look at the questions I wrote in the middle of the night. They remind me of Maude, but they make me think of Emily.

I realize I never asked Emily whether she knows how to ride a unicycle. But suddenly, the answer doesn't seem important.

I take out a thick black marker and cross out all four questions. Right underneath, I start a new list.

I plan to ask Emily the next time I see her. Whatever her answer turns out to be, I'm pretty sure it will be eleven times more interesting than whatever I'd come up with on my own.

I reach for the shelf and grab

Volume 58:

What Happens Next.

It's the last book in the series—the last time we hear from Annabelle Adams.

As the story begins, Annabelle is straddling two motorcycles that are roaring along on either side of an extremely narrow canyon that is just about to get a lot wider.

It ends with
Annabelle getting
knighted by the Queen of
England and trying to decide
whether to keep on solving
mysteries or to retire and spend
the rest of her life appearing on talk
shows and waving from parade floats.

Her wrist is starting to hurt from signing so many autographs. But her heart continues to ache from the injustice she sees every time she opens her eyes.

Which does she choose? The book doesn't say. *But I know.* Annabelle goes on and on. Because solving problems is in her bones. Because the world needs people like her and me . . . and Milton.

I walk down the hall to my brother's room. He is busy reading.

I reach into my pocket and take out the  pin that Maude left behind when she moved to California. I pin it onto Milton's pajamas.

It looks so official, he says, getting up and walking over to look at himself in the mirror.

That's because it is, I say. It's the real deal. Just like you.

Milton gives a little smile and then returns to his reading. I head back to my room. Tomorrow is the first day of winter vacation. If past years are any indication, Milton and I will have our work cut out for us. Missing sleds, mysterious snowballs, troublesome visiting cousins. The town will need the detectives of M&M Inc. to be at full strength.

And so I turn off my reading lamp.

But just down the hallway,
I can see that Milton's is still
burning bright.

THE END

MOXIE'S OFFICIAL DEBRIEF

As Annabelle Adams will tell you, every great detective learns from her mistakes. And so, at the end of every case, I like to look back and see what I did right and what I could have done better. If you would be willing to help me think through these questions, I would surely appreciate it.

1. What mistakes did I make throughout the day? What should I do to keep from making them again?
2. What can I do to become an even better detective moving forward? (Other than read Annabelle Adams books over and over and over.)
3. What made Principal Jones decide to give Milton the Eddie Award? Do you think it was the right decision?
4. If I really want to win the Eddie Award next term, what can I do to improve my chances?
5. What made Tracy Dublinger want to steal Eddie? I still can't quite figure it out. Can you? Should she get in trouble for what she did?
6. Is Emily Estevez a good best friend candidate for me? What makes someone a good friend?
7. I think I was a good big sister today, but I wonder if there is still some room for improvement. What could I do to be an even better sister to Milton?
8. Why is January?

HELLO!

We are Matthew Swanson and Robbi Behr.

Matthew likes to jog and play harmonica. Robbi likes to not jog and eat ice cream. Matthew was born at the base of a dormant volcano. Robbi was born with a bad attitude, but we're working on that.

We're married and we like each other and we spend our days making stuff together, usually stuff with Matthew's words and Robbi's drawings. But we sometimes make spaghetti and waffles and children. We have four children. The children eat the waffles.

We live in the hayloft of an old barn in Maryland, two blocks from the house where Robbi grew up. There is a trapdoor beneath the living room rug. There is a trapeze hanging from one of the beams. The children swing on the trapeze.

There's a clock tower in town that gongs every hour. There's a river nearby where we go to feed ducks. There's a bakery next door, and on open-window days we squirm and suffer all day long as the smell of bread and cookies floats in through the window.

For thirteen years, we made books on our own and trimmed and stapled and bound them by hand on our dining room table. Then a lady named Erin from a triangular building in New York asked us to make some books with *her*. She fed us fancy doughnuts, and so we said okay.

TRUTH! NONFICTION! HEAVILY RESEARCHED!

A BOOK ABOUT SEEING & SHARING

In summers, we fly 4,400 miles to the Alaskan tundra, where there are no roads or stores or flushing toilets. Robbi catches sockeye salmon with a 100-yard net. The kids make forts in the alders. Matthew makes macaroni and chases the grizzlies away.

Matthew enjoyed writing *The Real McCoys* because, deep down, he is an overconfident-but-insecure 10-year-old girl. Robbi enjoyed illustrating it because, deep down, she is a patient-and-observant 7-year-old boy.

Conclusion: We seem to do best when we stick together.

To get on our mailing list, browse our other books, find our blog, or schedule us to speak at (or Skype with) your conference, library, or school, visit us at

WWW.ROBBIANDMATTHEW.COM

Thanks for reading!

Matthew & Robbi

I love words. They make your brain bigger and the world more interesting and puzzles so much easier to solve. Here are a few terms that every detective should know.

CYBORG: A person with robotic enhancements, such as a superbrain, retractable eyebrows, or rocket-powered elbows. I am probably at least a little bit cyborg.

DIGNIFIED: Something or someone that is so proper and formal that people take it seriously. Me, for example.

DIPLOMAT: Someone whose job is to negotiate secret (and unsecret) treaties with other countries. Diplomats are usually rather dignified.

ENTOMOLOGIST: My mom's job. She is a scientist who studies insects and is an extraordinary human being.

FLOURISH: A bold or extravagant gesture—basically anything I do.

FORMIDABLE: Inspiring fear or respect by being impressively large, powerful, intense, or capable. The definition of this word in the *Oxford English Dictionary* should have a picture of me next to it.

GO FOR THE JUGULAR: The jugular is the very large (and very important) vein in your neck. Which is why certain argumentative animals try to bite each other in the jugular. For dignified detectives, to "go for the jugular" means to speak really loudly when questioning suspects.

HAPPENSTANCE: Another word for "coincidence," which is another word for "happening at the exact same time as something else for no apparent reason."

HEIRLOOM: A valuable something or other that has been handed down from one family member to the next through various generations. If my grandma were to give me her dentures and I were to give them to my own granddaughter, they would be an heirloom. More often, heirlooms are china plates or gaudy pins or fancy, old-fashioned clocks that kids are not allowed to touch.

HUMANITY: Another word for the human race, which includes you and me and, sadly, even Tracy Dublinger.

IRONCLAD: Literally, this means covered in iron, as old wooden ships used to be so that cannonballs would not blast holes in their sides. But it also means very strong or inflexible or incapable of being changed or broken—like my devotion to avocados.

MOTIVE: Someone's reason for doing something, especially when the reason is hidden or not obvious, as was the case when Tracy smiled so that everyone was forced to look at her perfect white teeth.

NUNCHUCKS: Amazing ninja weapon consisting of two sticks attached by a short chain or rope. I do not own nunchucks but absolutely should, even though my mom and dad do not agree.

OXFORD ENGLISH DICTIONARY: The biggest dictionary in the world, containing more than 300,000 words and 21,000 pages in 20 volumes, which is, admittedly, not quite as impressive as the Annabelle Adams series.

PEDIATRIC ONCOLOGIST: A doctor who treats kids with cancer—which is what Maude wants to be when she grows up.

RENEGADE: Someone who acts in a way that goes against the customs and beliefs of one's country, dojo, or elementary school.

RICOCHET: To bounce off of something and change direction. Not to be mistaken for my friend Rick O'Shea.

SCOTLAND YARD: The headquarters of the London Metropolitan Police, home to the most highly trained detectives in all of England. Annabelle once visited there on a vacation with her family and ended up staying for six months, learning all their secrets and teaching them a thing or two about hypnotizing bears.

SELFLESS: Someone who is more concerned with the needs of others than they are for their own. Principal Jones thinks Milton is selfless. And I have to agree.

SINGLE-HANDEDLY: When you do something without help from anyone else. Surprisingly, you can use two hands to do something single-handedly—as long as both of the hands are yours. Weird.

SMOKING GUN: A piece of evidence that is so convincing that, once you find it, the crime is basically solved. Like when the cookies are missing and little bits of snickerdoodle are all over your brother's hands and face.

TURN THE OTHER CHEEK: When, instead of fighting back after someone does something rude or mean to you, you remind yourself that two wrongs don't make a right and do nothing instead. Surprisingly, you can "turn the other cheek" without actually moving your head. Double weird.

UTOPIAN: Something that is really, really great or maybe even perfect. In a utopian version of Tiddlywhump, there would be no Dublingers and Mrs. Bunyan would never, ever talk about teeth.

READ THE REST OF MY (EVER-EXPANDING) DICTIONARY AT
REALMCCOYSBOOK.COM/MOXIES-DICTIONARY

Chapter 1: Cats Don't Do Yoga

Annabelle Adams was thinking about summer when she noticed a cat doing yoga on a bench outside her classroom window.

What the——? she thought.

She looked again. It was an orange cat, a friendly-looking fellow. Of course, the cat was not actually doing yoga. Because cats don't do yoga. Cats lounge and stretch and look at you with skepticism.

Annabelle's cat, Ellen, was the world's most capable cat. And even Ellen did not do yoga.

Only sixteen more minutes, thought Annabelle, glancing at the clock, biding her time. It was the last day of school before summer vacation. The students had already finished their last assignments.

But instead of giving up and letting everyone goof off for the rest of the day, Mr. Potter was lecturing about the importance of waiting a full hour after lunch before jumping into the pool.

Now it was 3:15, which meant only nine hundred seconds until Annabelle would be free to go back to doing what she loved best, which was reading books about adventure, practicing evasive maneuvers on her bicycle, and running through the obstacle course in her backyard. Annabelle did not know why she loved these things. She just loved them. And so she did them at every opportunity.

Annabelle already knew all about water safety (she was a certified junior lifeguard), and so she glanced out the window again. There were two cats now. And they were standing on hind legs, dancing together, ballroom style.

Annabelle looked around to see if anyone else was noticing this. But everyone else was squirming or sleeping or shoving or writing notes or reading fun books hidden inside of boring ones.

No one was listening to Mr. Potter. And no one seemed aware that five cats were now standing shoulder to shoulder on top of a minivan, doing alternating high kicks as if they were performing on Broadway.

Annabelle raised her hand. "Excuse me," she said before Mr. Potter could even call on her. "Something highly unusual is happening outside."

In an instant, everyone was up from their desks and racing to the window.

"Those cats are acting weird!" said Jim Jackson.

Jim usually said things like "BLERGL!" "KUGGA!" and "FART, FART, FART!" but this time, he had a point.

"Now, now!" said Mr. Potter. "Everyone sit down." But then he actually looked out the window and said, "Oh my."

There was nothing else to say. Fifteen cats were balanced on one another's shoulders in a perfect cat pyramid. The cat on top was holding one paw over his heart, as if he were saying the Pledge of Allegiance.

"I'm sorry, but I need to get to the bottom of this," said Annabelle, who sometimes felt called by a sense of duty so strong she couldn't contain it.

She raced into the hallway, which was already crowded. Apparently, others had noticed the cats and were equally concerned or excited by what was happening outside.

Soon pretty much everyone was in the schoolyard, standing in a great big circle around dozens of cats that were marching in neat rows, meowing an exciting song while pretending to play miniature trombones.

The teachers were trying their hardest to keep things under control, but it was impossible. This was the most exciting thing they had ever seen, and eventually the teachers gave up and joined in oohing and aahing and laughing and pointing and enjoying this marvelous display in the beautiful early-summer sunshine.

That's when the cats started to meow "For He's a Jolly Good Fellow" in three-part harmony.

"My goodness," said Annabelle, who usually didn't use that kind of language. She wondered if she might be asleep, so she tried to wake herself up, but when that didn't work, she instead tried to focus on getting to the bottom of things.

When she wasn't busy writing legal briefs, Annabelle's mother would tell Annabelle that there is always a logical explanation, no matter how strange and magical something might seem.

Cats don't play trombones, thought Annabelle rationally. *Cats don't meow in three-part harmony.*

When he wasn't busy saving countless lives in the emergency room, Annabelle's father would tell her that when a bunch of people are standing around refusing to accept the reality of a situation, it was essential that at least one person stand up and point out the truth.

But what was the truth in this situation? Unless Annabelle's eyes were deceiving her, these cats were actually doing the moonwalk while exchanging enthusiastic high fives with the kindergartners.

One of the cats gestured with clapping paws as if to say, "Come on, people, clap along with us," and so everyone started clapping and singing and laughing.

Annabelle hated to be a pessimist, but something about the situation didn't smell quite right.

Wait a minute, she thought, taking a closer look at the cat who seemed to be in charge. *I know that cat.*

It was Mr. Jingles, a plump gray British shorthair that belonged to a family across the street from the school. Annabelle knew it was Jingles because of the shiny silver bell around his neck. Annabelle stopped to scratch Jingles's head on her way to school most mornings. She had scratched his head this morning. This morning, he had not been dancing or singing or giving high fives. He had been lounging on the porch steps like a cat.

Annabelle looked at Mr. Jingles. Mr. Jingles looked at her.

If Annabelle's eyes could speak, they would have said, "What are you up to, Mr. Jingles?" and Mr. Jingles's eyes would have said, "Don't you worry. You're about to find out."

The cats were coming to the end of a chorus and were now grouped into another enormous pyramid at the center of the circle of teachers and students. Mr. Jingles stood at the very top, waving an invisible cane and tipping an invisible top hat. The song ended, and everyone clapped.

Suddenly the cats stopped smiling, which was alarming enough. But then Mr. Jingles raised his paw and meowed what sounded to Annabelle like a countdown.

"Meow, meow, meow, meow, MEOW!"

On the final meow, every cat leaped—hissing, teeth gleaming, claws bared—into the crowd.

The next few seconds were bad. Cats scratching. Kids crying. Teachers howling. It was shocking and sudden and loud. "I knew it," said Annabelle's heart, which had a way of speaking for itself from time to time.

But there was no time to think about what was happening. A fluffy white Persian leaped straight at Annabelle, angry eyes bulging. With a sudden surge of instinct, Annabelle turned her body sideways as the cat sailed narrowly by and bounced off a picnic table.

"KUGGA," said Jim Jackson, moments before a feisty Russian Blue landed on his back and dug its claws into his shoulders.

"FART! FART! FART!" said Jim, and Annabelle couldn't disagree.

As the air filled with flying, angry cats in no mood to be reasoned with, Annabelle ducked and twisted with the dexterity of a professional dodgeball player, which she was not.

New cats kept arriving. There were literally hundreds of them now, hissing and scratching and scowling.

Mr. Jingles stood up on his hind legs and made perhaps the most horrible sound that Annabelle had ever heard, and suddenly the other cats all stopped doing what they were doing and looked at him instead.

Sensing an opportunity to escape, Annabelle's classmates and teachers ran screaming, and the cats did not chase them. The cats seemed interested in only one thing now. The cats seemed interested in Annabelle.

"Hey, now," said Annabelle, as hundreds of cats turned their heads in her direction and started creeping closer.

Annabelle hated to retreat, but she saw no other choice. Keeping both eyes on Mr. Jingles, she walked backward toward the far end of the school yard while trying to plan her escape.

If only I had a jet pack, she thought. *If only I could shoot lasers from my hands*. Annabelle often longed for a jet pack. And for various superpowers, hand lasers among them. But never so much as in this moment when every cat in the world (it seemed) was marching toward her with eyes of gleaming fury.

Annabelle weighed her options. She could not win this fight. She was hopelessly outnumbered. Running seemed foolish. She didn't want to turn her back on the cats. And so she tried reason.

"Mr. Jingles!" said Annabelle. "What about all those loving scratches? What about the occasional treat I've tossed your way?" (Annabelle had been known to give Mr. Jingles a treat from time to time.) "We go way back, you and I!"

But Mr. Jingles wasn't having it, and neither were any of his friends.

The pack was closing in. Annabelle feared the end was near.

"It has been a very good twelve years," she said to herself, while longing for at least one hundred more.

But then she heard a roaring engine and a blaring horn and a deafening screech, which scattered the cats for just a moment. A fast-looking, bright red sports car with a racing stripe and killer spoilers skidded up to the curb. A door opened. Weird blue mist poured out.

"Get in!" said a voice from inside. Annabelle couldn't see who the voice belonged to.

Of course, Annabelle's parents had told her many times about never getting into cars with strangers—regardless of the color of the car—and Annabelle well understood that on a normal day, this was extremely good advice.

But this is not a normal day, thought Annabelle, as she dove into the car with the grace and desperation of an extremely worried gazelle.

GOFISH

MATTHEW SWANSON AND ROBBI BEHR

Do you have any strange or funny habits? Did you when you were a kid?
R: There is nothing strange or funny about my habits. But I can tell you all about Matthew's. For one thing, he covers his right ear whenever he blows his nose.
M: That's because I have a hole in my right eardrum! If I don't plug my ear when I blow my nose, my ear whistles. But it also means I can blow bubbles through my ear when I'm underwater.

If you could live in any fictional world, where would it be?
M: It's a world in which my stomach is the size of an Olympic-sized swimming pool. And there is an unlimited supply of burritos, pizza, and cheesecake. Cholesterol is nonexistent, and I have a lot of free time.
R: Ooh, can I join you in that world?
M: Sorry, I'm not sure there would be enough burritos, pizza, and cheesecake for both of us.
R: I thought you said there was an unlimited supply.
M: I did. But I'm still not sure that would be enough.

What's the best advice you've ever received about writing or making art?

R: The best advice I ever got about drawing was "Stop thinking about it!" which I didn't really understand at the time. I thought it meant "Get to it. You're wasting time!" But, after years of being an illustrator, I've come to realize that if I turn off my (overly critical) brain and just let myself draw, it leaves a lot more space for fun and surprising things to happen. It was great advice, but I still struggle to follow it.

M: My advice about writing is, never stop doing it. You are going to be terrible when you start writing because writing is so hard, but if you stick with it, you will get better and better throughout your entire life. I'm so glad I'm not a professional basketball player because eventually their knees stop working and they have to stop doing the thing they love. But whether or not my knees work, I'll be able to keep writing because you don't need your knees to write.

R: Unless you write with your knees. So my other best advice is, don't write with your knees.

M: Excellent point.

R: The other reason Matthew is glad he's not a professional basketball player is that he's terrible at basketball.

M: That point is not excellent. But, sadly, it's true.

What's your most embarrassing childhood memory?

M: Oh that's easy. It has to be in sixth grade when I stapled my finger to the floor. Or maybe it was in tenth grade when I was in a play and accidentally set myself on fire onstage. But probably it was when I was in a musical in ninth grade and went into the bathroom and practiced my solo right before it was time to go onstage, but my microphone was already turned on and the entire auditorium heard me singing and doing the other things you do in a bathroom.

R: Oh man. I've blocked most of mine out. But I remember once I was walking down an empty hallway in middle school and felt something dragging behind me. I looked down and discovered that there was an old pair of underpants sticking out of my pants leg.

M: That sounds even worse than stapling your finger to the floor.

R: It felt like being set on fire.

What was your favorite thing about school?

R: Honestly, it's the sound of a kickball being kicked really hard inside a gym. It goes booooiiiinnnng!

M: That is so specific! I love that.

R: I didn't realize when I was a kid that kickballs could be acquired anywhere else in the world. I thought they were something that belonged in a gym that only gym teachers could purchase. That sound still fills me with joy.

What is your favorite word?

R: *Borborygmus.* Which means the grumbling of your stomach.

M: My favorite word might be *obstreperous,* which means "noisy and difficult to control."

R: Ooh. I love it. It sounds just like what it means.

M: Synonyms include *unmanageable, disorderly, uncontrollable,* and *Robbi.*

R: I see what you did there.

How did you celebrate publishing your first book?

M: When the box containing the first copies arrived, I refused to open it. I didn't want the moment to be over, so I just kept it on my desk for a week. When we finally opened the box, I cried, and then we drove to a different town to eat delicious corned beef sandwiches. Some moments in life are so wonderful that I don't even want them to happen because once they do, they're over.

R: It's so hard to be Matthew.

What was your first job?

M: I was a clerk at a gourmet deli. You know what I loved about that job?

R: You got to eat everything and nobody knew?

M: *I got to eat everything and nobody knew!* I'm not sure that place survived the Matthew Swanson era, with all the lost inventory.

R: My first job was being a commercial fisherman with my family. It might also have been my worst job.

Did you play sports as a kid?

R: I did. I played lots of sports. I loved sports. I was a sporty-sports sporterson.

M: I tried. I really did. My dad signed me up for T-ball. And I really struggled to get the ball off the tee, because it required me to swing the bat parallel to the ball, which I found extremely difficult. After many failed attempts, I hit the ball with sufficient aim and force to get it off the tee.

R: Congratulations!

M: And then I ran to third base.

R: You got a triple? Well done.

M: No, I ran *directly* to third base. *Back*ward. That was my last day of T-ball.

R: It's so hard to be Matthew.

Moxie and Milton are total opposites—
but that might just be what
helps them solve their next case!

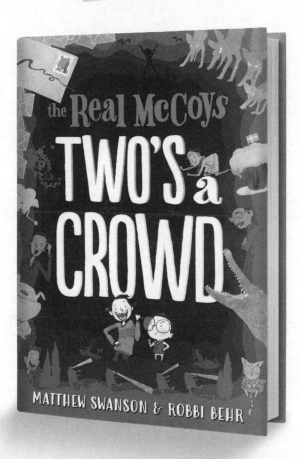

the Real McCoys
TWO'S a CROWD

MATTHEW SWANSON & ROBBI BEHR

KEEP READING FOR AN EXCERPT.

CHAPTER 1: THE SECRET HANDSHAKE

"The name's Moxie. Moxie McCoy."

You may know me by my deeds, which are legendary. You might be startled by my speed and smarts and lightning-quick reflexes, which are, quite frankly, unrivaled. You probably haven't heard of my puny little brother, Milton, but here he is, stuck to my side, like a leprechaun chasing a rainbow.

To the untrained eye, it might look like we're walking to school, but we are, in fact, working. On the lookout for peril, mishap, and disaster. Ready to save the world at a moment's notice.

MY hero and mentor, Annabelle Adams, Girl Detective, is only twelve years old, but she has saved the world 58 times already, once for each book in her series, which I have read 39¾ times and can recite to you from memory with one hand tied behind my back and the other one eating an apple.

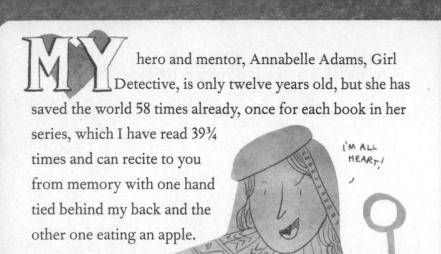

I'M ALL HEART!

After saving our school and solving the crime of the century, Milton and I are in search of a bigger, trickier, more death-defying challenge.

But for days and weeks, the world has been boringly normal. No capers! No heists!

NOT EVEN A MISSING LUNCH BOX!!!

As we turn the corner, the magnificent shape of 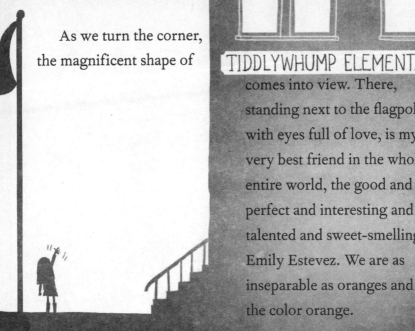 TIDDLYWHUMP ELEMENTARY comes into view. There, standing next to the flagpole with eyes full of love, is my very best friend in the whole entire world, the good and perfect and interesting and talented and sweet-smelling Emily Estevez. We are as inseparable as oranges and the color orange.

I have not talked to Emily for *three whole days* because she has been camping with her family in a cabin that does not have a phone.

We face each other, stick out our elbows, and do the most intricate-and-difficult-to-learn-or-duplicate secret handshake in the history of best-friendship.

Its many moves include "dump the soup," "love the slug," and "chop the avocado," because, as everyone knows but so few are willing to admit, soup is awful, slugs are incredibly lovable, and guacamole is the world's most perfect appetizer.

Secret Handshake

TAP THE ELBOWS

DUMP THE SOUP

LOVE THE SLUG

CHOP THE AVOCADO

SCOOP THE ICE CREAM

BUMP THE BUTT

GOBBLE THE TURKEY

BRUSH IT OFF

DO THE FUNGO

Emily agrees with me on all three points, but that is not why I love her. I love her because in the middle of her soul is a **BALL of GOODNESS** so warm and full and perfectly round that you could use it to play golf if you liked playing golf, which I don't.

A group of kids has gathered to watch our handshake. When we finish, we get a round of applause, which we ignore, because now it's time for a long, enjoyable hug.

CLAP CLAP CLAP CLAP CLAP CLAP CLAP CLAP CLAP CLAP CLAP

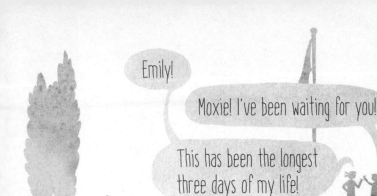

Emily!

Moxie! I've been waiting for you!

This has been the longest three days of my life!

I need your help with something,

says Emily. I can tell from her expression that something serious is going on. Which is rather exciting.

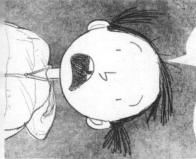

What is it? Has your cousin been kidnapped? Are your jewels missing?

No, everyone's fine. And I don't have any jewels. But I might have a case for you!

My eyes get big. My heart gets wide. Emily knows I've been on the lookout for the next big case.

TELL ME!!